MAKING THE LOVE LIST

TALL DARK & DRIVEN~BOOK ONE

BARBARA DELEO

FOREWORD

This book was previously published, in part, as The Bouquet List

CLAIM YOUR FREE NOVELLA.

Waiting on Forever—Alex's story—is the prequel to this *Tall, Dark and Driven* series and is available **exclusively** and **FREE** for subscribers to my reader list.

Details on how to claim your **FREE** novella are at the back of this book.

1

"*D*o you have an invitation, miss? Only wedding guests can come in at this time of night."

The lanky young boy in an oversize doorman's uniform stepped into Yasmin Katsalos's path at the gates of the Aegean Palace, the wedding hall her parents had owned in Brentwood Bay for the past forty years. Behind him, well-dressed guests milled about in the courtyard while boys in miniature suits and girls in princess dresses chased each other in the soft light of dusk. The rich aroma of spit-roast lamb carried on the breeze, and the familiar sound of a jaunty bouzouki band played in the distance.

Yasmin finally let herself sigh in dizzy relief. She was home, and there was a time only a few weeks ago when she'd thought she might never see this place, or her parents, again.

Pulling her gaze from the wedding scene, she peered closer at the guard. "Stratis, is that you?" She dropped her backpack and threw her arms around her father's young godson. "You've gotten so big!" She laughed. "And when did you start working here? Last time I saw you was in the Greek school Christmas pageant playing a palm tree!"

Stratis stood stiff beneath her hug and when she leaned back, his eyes widened. "No, I don't believe it! Yas? Oh my God. I didn't recognize you with your ... your *hair* and ... the nose stud. And when did you stop wearing glasses?"

Yasmin touched the purple streaks in her glossy black hair. Not purple exactly, more a rich, deep lilac, almost the exact shade of the amethyst deceiver, the little mushroom she was so fond of, and the irony made her smile. There'd be no more amethyst deceiver in her near future, and the thought of that, and her whole new look, caused her heart to do a half pike, double backflip.

The hair and the nose stud were the first two items on her bouquet list, the list of things she wanted to do in her life after surviving dengue fever in Borneo, and she couldn't wait to get started on the rest. Putting her PhD on hold was third, and learning a new language was at four. Seducing a tall, dark man out of her league was five. Some things on her list scared her more than others, but she'd have attempted none of them in her quiet and conservative old life BD—before dengue.

Now everything was different.

A fluffy black and white cat emerged from the shadows and began to rub itself against her shins. "I've been doing research work in Borneo for a little bit, but I'm back earlier than I'd planned, so I thought I'd surprise Mom and Dad. Are they around?"

Stratis shook his head. "Your mom's not here, and the last time I saw Mano he was in the restaurant threatening to fire one of the new waiters for wearing his pants too low. Want me to take your bag upstairs while you go find him?"

She bent down to stroke the cat. "Upstairs?"

He nodded toward the nearest building. "Your mom and dad moved into the old apartment a while back so they could rent their house as part of the wedding package. You didn't know?"

Her chest hollowed. She'd been in Borneo for eighteen months, but her parents hadn't mentioned anything about moving to the apartment. Things had been tough at the Palace for a while now, which was part of the reason she hadn't told them she'd been so sick, but she hadn't realized things had gotten this bad.

"No, I didn't know they'd moved. Thanks for taking my bag, Stratis. I'll go look for Dad and catch you later."

Stratis picked up her backpack and, with the cat trotting after him, headed up the stairs to the apartment that over-looked the entranceway. She walked through the courtyard and everything was as she remembered. Statues of Greek gods were dotted around the perimeter, while a pink fountain in the middle changed its colored light to synchronize with the movement of the water. If she hadn't just traveled in a cab from the airport, she could be fooled into thinking she was in Greece. Well, maybe Greece in the 1980s. The decor had never quite kept in step with the decades, but there was more to it this time. Some of the bright turquoise and yellow pots that held tumbling geraniums and basil in every available space were cracked, and the whitewashed wall covered in brilliant purple bougainvillea was peeling. Whether the decor hadn't been modernized because there wasn't enough money, or the other way around, the Aegean Palace wasn't what it used to be. This sight, combined with the news that her parents had moved into the apartment, made Yasmin even more anxious to find her father.

If she weren't in such a hurry, she'd have gone to say hello to Monty, the parrot who was just as much of an institution as the Dionysus mosaic on the ground and the plastic grapevines adorning the front of the restaurant. There would be time to chat to Monty later, but right now she couldn't wait to see her dad.

As soon as she entered the restaurant in its conglomeration of gold and black decor, she spotted him. He was standing with his back to her, arms flailing wildly as he harangued a waiter in Greek. The emotion she'd kept bottled inside the last few weeks overpowered her, and she rushed up behind and threw her arms around him. "*Baba!*"

"*Panagia!*" he called out and spun around. Then, just like Stratis, he froze. "Yasmin! *Kori*, is that you?"

Instead of squeezing her close in one of his bear hugs that she'd missed so much, he took a step back and his horrified gaze swept from the top of her head, to the diamond glinting in her nose, and down to the Doc Marten boots she wore on her feet. And then to her dismay, his eyes filled with tears.

"It's okay, Dad," she said in a rush. "I should've told you. Something happened in Borneo and I wanted a fresh ..."

He cut her off before she could deliver the speech she'd prepared on the plane about how the fever had affected her, how the list she'd written was changing her already. She should've known that seeing her like this would be a shock.

"It's your mother," her father choked.

"Mom? What's happened? Where is she? Is she okay?"

Her father's enormous chest rose, then fell, beneath his tight black waistcoat. "She has gone to Greece." He vigorously crossed himself. "And thanks be to *Panagia* that you have come to help me bring her back," he said, swiping at his eyes. He dropped his voice as if he was suddenly conscious of his outburst. "Come to the back office and I will explain everything."

While the wedding crowd began to move inside for what was probably the arrival of the bride and groom, Yasmin followed her father across the courtyard and into one of the offices. Her mother was in Greece without him? That had never happened before. A relative must've fallen ill. Perhaps her mother's sister, Maria. Her parents had run this place for forty years, but she couldn't imagine her father coping on his own. Especially when times were so tough.

When they were seated in the office, Mano cleared his throat and stroked his salt-and-pepper mustache. "Your mother doesn't believe in the Aegean Palace anymore."

Yasmin blinked, trying to make sense of what he'd just said. "What do you mean? Mom loves this place."

"Things have been very tough. Those Pattersons. *Pah! Pah!*" He paused and pretended to spit twice over his shoulder. "Those criminals steal so much of our business and I promise your mother that I will turn things around. She shouts at me and tells me this is another one of my schemes with the hairy brain and that she will not return until either this place is sold, or the pigs have flown and it starts to make money again. And then she just orders a cab and leaves. She does not understand that I borrowed the money for the renovations so the Palace can finally be successful."

Yasmin drew a breath and reached for her father's hand. "Have you told Nick and Ari?"

Mano's face paled further. "Your brothers know your mother has gone to Greece, but they don't know the whole story and they mustn't. I will not have their careers spoiled because your mother has her crazy thoughts."

"What about the money from the sale of Yiayia's house? Didn't that help things a bit?" Yasmin's heart squeezed at the memory of her grandmother, who'd only died a month before.

"Of course, your brother bought the old house to sell it to your cousin Alex's girlfriend. He paid a lot of money, but then it was divided in three between your mom, your uncle Leo, and aunt Maria, and it hardly made a difference when we used it to pay off some debt. I will go to Lesbos tomorrow to bring her back and then it will all be forgotten."

"You're leaving tomorrow? Who'll run things?"

"I've explained everything to Grace, and she has it all in hand. And Lane is doing the renovation, of course."

"Lane Griffiths?" She knew of Grace, the wedding planner for the Palace, but she hadn't seen Nick's best friend for years. "Wait, what? A renovation?"

"Yes. Lane is a good boy and he is very successful with so many restaurants."

"And you're giving him full license to do what he wants while you're away?" None of this made sense. "Why not get Nick and Ari to help out as well?"

"I've asked Lane to help redesign the restaurant and the menu, so people start booking with us instead of those dirty Pattersons. Your brothers are busy enough with their own lives. They don't need this worry as well."

"*Kyrie* Katsalos." A young waiter had poked his head around the door and the look on his face suggested he was afraid it might be chopped off. "That new boy has dropped the wedding cake on the floor and the mother of the bride has fainted."

"*Panagia mou!*" Mano shouted and lifted both arms to the heavens. "What have I done to deserve this madness?

6

These crazy people! No wonder my Pia wants to leave and go back to peaceful island life."

The waiter was gone in an instant and when Mano dropped his hands he picked up a pair of glasses, held them up to his face, and squinted at Yasmin. "You can't be working here with that hair and that thing in your nose. We have standards to maintain. Grace is good with the Greek mothers, but they will be nervous that your mother isn't here, so you will need to soothe them. And not look like a *karagiozis* from the carnival."

"*Baba*, I need to tell you something." He wouldn't understand any of the things on her list, but she at least needed to tell him she'd been sick.

He dropped the glasses and rummaged through the pile of papers on the desk. "Not now, *koukla*. You can tell me everything when I bring your mother home by the end of the week. Where is that damned to God airplane ticket? I'm getting an early uber in the morning. Do whatever Lane asks and let me know if there are any problems. I will give you his number so you can meet, and he can explain what he has planned." He stood up. "Now I must go and clean Mrs. Konstantinopolous and that wedding cake off the floor." He walked around the desk and kissed her on both cheeks. "You are a good girl, and I know you'll make me proud," he said on his way out the door.

He hadn't even asked why she was back. Or how long she was staying. And she didn't even want to think about the fact that he thought her brothers "had busy enough lives" but that she'd just do what was asked of her.

How could she fulfill her list when he expected her to fit right back into the role of a good daughter? And if she had to stay and supervise things while her father was away, she would certainly not "do whatever Lane asks". She'd been telling her parents for years the Palace needed to be dragged kicking and screaming into the twenty-first century. She had her own ideas how to go about it.

At eleven o'clock the next morning, Yasmin stood in the doorway of an old English tea shop and inhaled the scent of fresh-baked goodies. What did Lane look like now? She'd phoned him and left a message to meet her here to discuss what they were going to do about the Palace. He'd always been an earnest boy when he was younger, focused and serious like her brother Nick, always aloof and a bit superior —the sort of kid you'd expect to see carrying a briefcase to his own wedding. But there had always been something completely mesmerizing about him as well—his piercing eyes, his knowing smile; just a glance her way when she was a girl and she'd been a puddle of teenage crush.

As her eyes became accustomed to the low light in the tearoom, she stopped still. Was that him? A dark-haired guy in a charcoal suit sat at a booth in the back, but he hadn't noticed her. He was too busy looking at a laptop screen, his brow creased and his fist slowly tapping his chin.

He had a strong profile, a jaw that curved in a tight arc, and skin the burnished tan of honey. His dark brown hair reminded her so strongly of someone that she had a sudden sense of déjà vu but couldn't quite pin down who it was.

When she took a step into the room, he looked up, and in that instant her heart skipped a beat. Her pulse quickened, her palms became clammy, and she had to remind herself to put one foot in front of the other. The past came tumbling back, and for a moment it felt as though she were transported back in time, unable to speak when he was near. Back then he'd hardly acknowledged she existed, and now he was looking directly at her.

He stood at the booth, his head nearly touching the light hanging above him before he stepped forward. "Yasmin," he said. "It's been a long time." Goosebumps flew across her arms and raced up the back of her neck. His voice was low and slow, the hypnotizing tone of a late-night radio host talking only to her while she was lying alone in her bed …

Stop it!

"Thanks so much for meeting me here," she said, trying to appear cool and collected. Moving closer, her gaze rested on his, and she held out her hand at the same time that he dipped his face to kiss her cheek. In a clash of fine suit cloth and fingers, her hand collided with his stomach as his lips touched her ear when she twisted her face in surprise. A blush started to burn its way across her cheeks, but without looking at him or acknowledging the blunder, she slid into the booth opposite, the brand of his lips still warm on her skin. "Thanks for meeting me here," she said as her eyes finally landed back on his face, before she realized she was repeating herself. "There's a wedding on at the Palace today and I didn't want to get under everyone's feet. It was all a bit of a surprise when Dad told me about leaving for Greece last night."

He sat too and regarded her with his head tilted slightly to the side. *Those piercing blue eyes.* "I never would've recognized you."

She let out a nervous laugh that sounded all schoolgirl breathless and was glad to find the waiter ready to take their order.

His brow creased and he looked at her more intently. "Are you okay? You've gone all red."

She loosened the neckline of her new Chinese-collar

dress and cleared her throat. She picked up the menu and flicked through it, glad of an excuse to look away. "Fine ... I'm fine, thanks. A pot of tea, please," she said to the waiter who'd appeared beside her. "And is that scones I can smell?"

"Sure is. Right out of the oven. Would you like one with jam and cream?"

Her stomach gurgled in anticipation. "Yes, please."

"Black coffee for me, thanks," Lane said and pushed his computer aside. "Interesting place." He looked around as the waiter left.

Yasmin clasped her hands on the table. "Since the coffee in Borneo wasn't the best, I got used to drinking tea. There are so many different kinds there. You can have Chinese tea, iced milk tea, lemon tea. There's even one called pulled tea made with condensed milk."

He blinked. She was actually scaring him with her blathering. "Isn't this place cute? My uncle Leo, our cook, told me about it."

He twisted the other way, then fixed his gaze back on her. "It has ... atmosphere. It's all a bit dark and dreary as if it's the middle of an English winter outside."

Of course, he was an expert on restaurants; maybe this had been a bad choice.

"So, how have you been?" she said breezily. "Dad said you've got a great chain of restaurants."

"Had." He still looked as serious and aloof as she'd remembered, and his intense stare still made the skin on the back of her neck tingle. "I've just sold them and have a very large project starting in a couple of months."

"What's that?"

"I was given the opportunity to create my signature restaurant in the newest Prescott Hotel. It's the sort of thing

I'd always had as an ultimate goal but didn't think I'd achieve until my mid-thirties."

"*The* Prescott Hotels? I've heard that guy's ruthless."

"He is, but he picked my restaurant out of a pretty impressive lineup, so I'm ready to put everything into it. Doing this job for your dad was good timing because the hotel won't be ready until the end of summer, and I hate not working."

She tucked a piece of hair behind her ear. "Look, I know Dad asked you to oversee the changes, but now that I'm here I can take over."

He frowned as if she'd asked him to embezzle money from his grandma, but still spoke with that voice as smooth as liquid chocolate. "Your dad asked me to do a little more than advise on decor, Yasmin. He asked that I manage the finances and oversee all the restaurant changes. Trust me, it's easy to pay thousands of dollars for very little impact, and he wants his investment maximized. And with all due respect, you haven't had industry experience."

She put her palms flat on the table and straightened her spine. He didn't need to know why she was back, or that she'd been sick. He just needed to know that she was going to be in charge of this project, get creative, and help her parents at the same time.

"I appreciate your experience and expertise," she said, making herself look directly in his eyes, "but I really want to do this on my own, so we can tell Dad we're checking in from time to time and leave it at that."

"Your hair," he suddenly said. "How do they get the purple on there when it's so dark underneath?"

She fingered the piece of hair over her shoulder, taken aback by his sudden interest in her. "They take a bit and bleach it, then when all the color's gone they put the purple over it."

"You mean they take all the existing color out completely? That must be damaging to the hair shaft. Does it ever recover?" He frowned again, and she had to suppress a chuckle at the look of concern on his face. He was just as she'd remembered, serious and aloof, and kinda out of touch with doing something for fun.

"I'm not really sure. I just had it done in Singapore on my way home."

"Interesting. I hope it doesn't cause permanent injury."

Crickets

Had he really just said that? Yasmin stifled a laugh at the irony of him worrying about damage to her hair when she'd just survived a life-threatening illness.

"As I was saying," Lane said, "you'll need advice and a detailed plan of what needs to be done. I have a designer who'll come by this week to advise on any structural changes, and then I'll have one of my chefs come in and we can take a look at a menu redesign. I also have …"

She blinked. "Hang on a minute."

"Yes?"

"I want to have some fun with this, make the most of the opportunity."

"Then I guess we'll need to talk with your dad. It's his money and his investment. He didn't indicate that the focus should be … fun." He lifted a strong shoulder, then let it fall.

Suddenly, Yasmin thought back to her early teens when she would dream about Lane taking notice of her, talking to her, and seeing her as someone important. He'd seemed untouchable back then—guys like him still were, for a girl who spent more time with mold than men. What would it be like to show him some fun? Give him a glimpse at a different side of life?

A strange feeling overtook her and her mouth dried.

Seduce a tall, dark, and mysterious man who's out of my league.

The sense of déjà vu—Lane Griffiths with his suit and his status and his cool aloofness, his strong shoulders and those heart-melting eyes—if she played her cards right, Lane Griffiths could be her number five!

2

*L*ane flicked his gaze away from Yasmin for the tenth time in the last two minutes. He didn't want her to think he was staring. He just couldn't believe that this stunning woman with the bright purple hair and the tiny diamond winking in her nose was his best friend Nick's kid sister. When she'd left a message this morning, he'd been expecting someone serious and intellectual, someone like the picture that Mr. and Mrs. Katsalos had on their front room dresser. The girl receiving her master's degree for some obscure science thing, with dark-rimmed glasses and an uncertain smile. He hardly remembered her when she was younger, other than that she was studious and a bit awkward, nothing like this sexy woman with the quirky grin and sparkling eyes.

What had happened to her? And what did she mean, 'fun'? This was business, pure and simple. Fun didn't factor in at all.

"Mano said it's imperative that the restaurant keep running while any changes are made," he said, to pull himself back to the matter at hand.

Yasmin nodded. "Dad says things are pretty tough financially. In the old days, he and Mom would be run off their feet in summer with two weddings a day sometimes, but Dad implied the rivalry with Patterson Weddings has gotten so bad that they've lost a lot of business."

She'd stopped refusing his help outright, so he decided to try to get her fully on board. "What sort of ideas do you have so far?"

She leaned forward, her chocolate eyes sparkling. He'd noticed a silver necklace with a butterfly moving against her throat. It danced each time she spoke, and he couldn't stop watching it, and imagining pressing a kiss on the skin beneath.

"We need to rethink everything from the menu to the decor," she said, and he focused on her dusky lips as she spoke. "Mom and Dad have always had good chefs, but they've tried to keep the food really traditional. Even the Greek families who get married at the Palace would love a more modern menu, I'm sure. And the same goes with the decor. Murals of Santorini and plastic grapevines hanging from the ceiling might've been stylish in the eighties, but not anymore."

He nodded. She'd been thinking carefully about this.

The waiter put their drinks down, placed a scone that resembled a small pillow with little plates of jelly and cream in front of Yasmin, and left.

"I have this idea for making the restaurant more communal," she said, pulling the plate with the scone toward her and beginning to tear it apart. Her eyes lit up. "We could redo the table design, or the layout." She spooned bright red jelly onto each half of the scone and then followed it with a dollop of cream. She smiled brightly.

"Would you like one of these? I've heard they're disgustingly delicious."

He shook his head as he watched her finish the job, then take a huge bite. She closed her eyes and made a low noise at the back of her throat that made him feel like he was intruding on a private moment, and he wanted to hear it over and over. "God, these are good," she said as her eyes opened and rested on him again, her voice muffled by scone. A thin line of whipped cream sat above her top lip before she carefully wiped it away with a finger. "And we could have the whole place look rustic but a lot more modern." She licked the cream from her finger, then chewed, and a ripple of need shuddered through him. A completely inappropriate reaction to the sister of his oldest friend.

He shook his head to clear it. *What was she saying? Tables, right.* He wanted to point out that was the most ridiculous idea he'd heard for a wedding venue ever but was mindful of the fact that the sooner he took control of this colorful, unguided missile, the better. "I don't know many people who'd want their wedding to be rustic."

"Oh." She took another sip of her tea, but her eyes held his. "You don't think people want to be more relaxed at a wedding these days?"

This might not be as easy as he'd assumed. There was so much hope in her eyes.

A bell sounded—a single melodic note—from her handbag, and her eyes swung to it, then back at him. The echo must've gone on for a full ten seconds.

"Important text?"

"No, not a text. I should've turned it off, though." She fished her phone from her bag, flicked a switch on the side, and shoved it back in.

"We can talk details later. Your dad has said he's

prepared to pay what it takes, but I've given him quite a conservative estimate at the moment," Lane said. "I don't think we want to be making wholesale changes without your parents' knowledge."

Yasmin lifted her chin and brushed crumbs from the corner of her moist mouth. "I spoke to Dad before he left this morning. He said to do whatever I could to get the restaurant humming again, both on the catering side and in the restaurant."

But her father couldn't afford anything too grand. Things were tough for Pia and Mano. Nick had mentioned it a couple of times. "I'm sure your parents will be selling soon, so these changes will be merely cosmetic."

Her mouth dropped and a look of horror passed across the smooth skin of her face. "Sell the Palace? No. They've built this business from nothing over forty years. It's their lifeblood, and the livelihood of people like my Uncle Leo. I want to do everything I can to try to turn things around for them."

He shrugged. "Conditions are tough, business has dropped off, and your mother has left for Greece. It doesn't make sense to throw a whole lot of money at renovating the restaurant if it's just going to be sold out from under you."

Her eyes became glossy, and he could've kicked himself. He'd said too much. Hurt her.

"Even if that were true, it'd be much better to sell when it was on the rise rather than floundering, wouldn't it?" she said. "It makes sense that while I've got the time and the passion I do whatever I can to help out. Overhauling the restaurant is something I think I can do."

Could she? Wasn't she doing a PhD or something at a university? As far as he knew, she had no experience with design or budgeting, and he didn't think Mano would be impressed if this ended up making things worse. But if he monitored her closely and kept her passion for self-expression and crazy ideas in check, it might work out. "Okay, but we'll need to be open with each other, have a realistic budget, and we need to work toward a relaunch date so we can incorporate it with branding for the wedding hall side of the business."

She nodded as her eyes shone and she lifted the scone, ready to take another bite. His stomach muscles clenched in anticipation of hearing her moan again. "How long do you think it would all take?"

"I'm free for the next month, and it's important we see changes before the summer wedding season is finished. We need easy and non-disruptive solutions. We'll work around the clock and at weekends, and we'll plan a relaunch party where we can invite influential event people, so they'll need enough notice. Hopefully by then your parents will be back."

"Dad thinks he can get Mom to come back in a week or so, but she must be pretty upset to have taken off like she did. I'm calling her tonight." With a finger, she scooped up the remaining cream on the plate and popped it in her mouth, her finger lingering on her lips.

He almost let out a groan of his own. "If you listen to my advice and we're both committed to working together to take the Aegean Palace to a whole new level just as your father wants, I think we can do it." Finally he tore his focus from her mouth, wondering how he could endure thirty days of this torture. Maybe he could make sure he wasn't around when she ate. Whipped cream especially.

After meeting with Lane, Yasmin called her best friend Genie, who'd arrived back from college in Florida last week. Genie squealed down the phone and said to come straight over. Yasmin jogged the last few blocks between the Palace and Genie's house, and she noticed how the town of Brentwood Bay had spread out. Much of this area had been countryside when her parents first built the Palace. There were still some green areas, and the summer sun dappled the sidewalk as she ran.

As Yasmin passed the redbrick Episcopal church, she thought about growing up here, how hard her parents had worked to make a life for them all after immigrating from Greece. They worked virtually seven days a week to make the wedding hall a success. Yasmin had spent a lot of time with her grandparents growing up and they'd been a tight family. Things must be pretty desperate for her mom to take off so suddenly, especially in the middle of wedding season, and she was looking forward to calling her tonight. Maybe if she knew Yasmin was back and could see the hard work they were putting into the renovation when she got home, she'd find a new happiness in the place that had meant so much to all of them.

She reached Genie's parents' house and walked up the steps. It didn't take her friend long to answer the door.

"*Oh my God!* You look unbelievable!" Genie said after they hugged, and she ushered Yasmin in. "Your hair! And that outfit! Holy shit, Yaz, what happened to you out there in the jungle?"

"You think the color's okay? You'd tell me if I look like the love child of Cruella de Vil and Barney, right? I had it done in Singapore, and Dad's reaction wasn't exactly enthusiastic."

"The color's amazing. You look like a cross between Lady

Gaga and Katy Perry—sexy, and a little bit wild and ..."
Genie slapped her palm to her chest, eyes wide. "Speaking
with all the love in my heart, honey ... nothing remotely like
the safe and staid Yasmin Katsalos I used to know."

After they walked into Genie's kitchen, Genie looked at
Yasmin from all sides, then pulled out two chairs at the
kitchen table and sat down. "But you are looking a bit too
skinny. They obviously don't have Ben & Jerry's Salted
Caramel in Borneo."

She hadn't had a chance to tell her father she'd been
sick, and she certainly wouldn't be telling Lane Griffiths, but
she wanted her best friend to know.

"I had dengue fever. The doctors weren't sure I would
make it. Mom and Dad don't know how bad things got, and
now that everything's happened with them I don't want to
tell them until they get back."

Genie sat closer. "Oh my God, that sounds awful. Are
you okay now?"

Yasmin nodded. "Apart from getting pretty tired, I'm fine.
My insurance company paid for me to see a specialist in
Singapore and he said that I should be good as new in a
couple of months. A bit of rest and I'll be back to my old
self. I guess this whole thing of having to stay at the Palace
'til Mom and Dad get back has worked in my favor. But that's
enough about me. How are you?"

Genie tilted her head to one side. "With the greatest
respect, Yas, if you came home to recover and get back to
your old self ... that new diamond stud in your nose and the
purple hair?"

Yasmin chuckled. "The old Yas is long gone, G. Staring
down death in that jungle hut, I promised myself that from
now on I'm going to live exactly the way *I* want, and
changing my hair color was the second thing on my

bouquet list." She touched the tiny stud in her nose. "And this bad girl was my first."

"Your whatsit list?"

"Bouquet list. You've heard of the old Jack Nicholson movie, right? *The Bucket List*? Two old guys who make a list of everything they want to do before they die. Well, when I was starting to recover, I wrote a list of the things I want to do now that I know I'm *not* going to die—my bouquet list."

Genie smiled. "Kinda cute given your parents own a wedding hall. Bucket for when you're kicking it, and bouquet when you're launching into something new ..." She nodded. "I like it. But having purple hair and a nose stud were your top priorities?"

Yasmin chuckled. "Kind of. You know me, I've been a good Greek daughter my whole life. I studied hard and did exactly what I was supposed to right from when I was little. When I realized how close to death I'd gotten in Borneo, I decided to live the way I want to—be the person I want to be, look the way I want to look, even if it scares the holy hell out of me."

Genie's mouth lifted in a teasing grin. "If I had your mom, I'd be glad she was out of the country when I got myself all dyed and pierced too. So, if the stud in your nose was first on your list, and having purple hair was second, what's number three?"

"Putting my PhD studies on hold. My doctor said I could potentially go back to college this semester, but I'm phoning my professor tonight to tell him I'm sitting this year out. I know he's going to be disappointed, but being so sick has kinda given me a hunger to see what else there is in life." She squeezed Genie's arm. "And a chance to spend more time with my best friend. Speaking of which, I'm so excited your brother invited me to his wedding. That's one bonus from having to come home. Now I can go if it's still okay. How's the countdown going?"

"Hideous," Genie said, shuddering and pulling a face. "Paul's fiancée, Carmel, is gorgeous, but her mother, Pat, is as overbearing and subtle as a cattle prod. Can you believe she said my blonde hair would clash with the yellow brides-maid's dress?" She clutched Yasmin's arm and looked stricken. "I'm really sorry the wedding's at the Patterson place. Paul would've much preferred to get married at the Palace, but Pat's in thick with Mrs. Patterson and I think he's a bit scared of her. He'll be so pleased you can make it."

Yasmin shrugged. "It's fine, honestly. We've been losing a lot of business to the Pattersons lately. Paul's wedding will give me a chance to have a sneak peek at what magic they're using to be so successful. Do you need help with getting anything ready?"

"I have a hair trial Tuesday. Wanna come to that?"

"I'd love to."

"So, what else is on this bouquet list of yours?" Genie asked. "Nude rodeo, fire eating?"

Yasmin counted on her fingers. "Learn a new language, seduce a tall, dark guy who's totally out of my league—"

"Oooh, I like that one," Genie exclaimed. "I guess there hasn't been a lot of time for seduction in the toadstool fields of Borneo."

Yasmin chuckled. "It feels like I've been chained to a desk in a sexless white lab coat since I was a teenager, and everyone else I know seems to have had a go at seduction. Who knows, maybe Lane Griffiths could fit the bill."

"Oh, Lane! Nick's old friend? The one we all had a crush on when we were fourteen. The cool, superior sort of one with the nice pecs."

Yasmin nodded. "Dad hired him to oversee renovations at the Palace."

"A bit of Lane Griffiths is sure to help your recovery. What's on the rest of your list?"

"Visit Rome, learn to dance, follow my heart and not my head, then find my artist lover in a country far away from here and spend the rest of our lives traveling, tied to nothing and no one. I haven't quite figured out how I'm going to finance any of this, but I'm definitely going to do my best to make it all happen."

Just as soon as I figure out how to get Lane to notice me.

At ten o'clock that night, Yasmin sat at the small table in her parents' apartment and opened her computer ready to speak to her mom in Greece. It was strange being in the apartment rather than the rambling house she'd grown up in. Things must be really bad financially for her parents to move in here and let out the house. Normally, they'd never talk to her about financial troubles and it was only that her dad was in such a state when she'd arrived that he'd let it slip. It strengthened her resolve to do her very best in this renovation to help turn things around for them.

It didn't feel right keeping the secret of the renovation from her mom, but she'd promised her dad before he left that he'd be the one to tell her.

She clicked on the FaceTime app and it connected. For a minute everything was fuzzy and then her mother's face came into sharp focus.

But it wasn't just her mother, it was her aunt Maria, her uncle Thassos, an old woman she'd never seen before, and a couple of kids as well. They all let out a simultaneous shriek.

"*Koukla!*"

"Mom! It's so good to see you." Yasmin laughed. "*Yiasou Theia, yiasou Theio!*"

There was more shrieking in Greek, and then everyone behind her mother waved.

"So it's true," her mother said, both hands at her cheeks. "You really are home, and your hair really is purple."

"Yes, I'm home. How are you? Are you okay? I've been worried about you."

"I'm okay. I'm going to Eressos soon to see Yiayia's sister Arianthe, so I had to call early. Why are you home? Your father seems to have no idea. All he could say when he called was that you had purple hair and you were wearing men's boots. Oh my, it's so good to see you. How are you? How are you feeling after that bug you got in Borneo?"

"I'm good. Great. Feeling much better. It's lovely to be home but I really miss you and dad. How are things in the village?"

Her mom's salt and pepper hair was loose around her face, the skin by her eyes crinkled. "Wonderful," she said. "Everything in the village feels so slow and easy. It's so lovely to see Maria and Thassos and the kids. It's been so nice to spend some time talking about Yiayia and showing everyone here the video of her funeral."

Yasmin's chest squeezed tight. One of the hardest things about being so far away in Borneo had been missing her grandmother's funeral back here. It was part of the reason that she'd downplayed how ill she'd been as her mom had so much to cope with back then.

"Did Nick tell you that he sold Yiayia's house to Alex's girlfriend, Mara? Yiayia would be so pleased to know that her neighbor ended up with that house that she loved so much."

Yasmin smiled. She hadn't caught up with her cousin Alex and his girlfriend Mara yet.

"They're supposed to be coming to the island, Alex and Mara. It will be lovely to see them. Oh, that reminds me. Have you seen Boris?"

"I haven't caught up with many of the staff yet. I'll make sure to check in with Grace tomorrow."

Her mother smiled. "No, Boris is Mara's cat. We're looking after him for a couple of months while they travel. Leo and Mila couldn't have him at their place because your aunt's allergic."

"Oh, the black and white cat? Yes, I saw him when I arrived yesterday, but I don't think he's been around since."

"He'll be down in the courtyard by the restaurant. Leo feeds him down there and he's put a basket in the utility room. Can you just check tomorrow?"

"Sure."

Her mother talked about her aunt and uncle in the village and the things they'd been up to but as soon as she had the opportunity, Yasmin spoke. "What happened, Mom? Why did you decide to go back to Greece without Dad? And why not tell Nick and Ari what was happening?"

Her mom rested her chin on her hands and was quiet for a moment, then she blew out a breath. "It's so hard to explain, honey. I don't know when I decided I needed to get away. Maybe Yiayia's death was a catalyst, but to be honest, things have been pretty difficult for a while."

"Between you and Dad?"

"Yes, but that's primarily because business has been so tough. I just got sick of your dad's promises, his optimism that we'd be able to turn things around. When it became clear that none of you kids were going to take over at the Palace, I just got tired of working harder and harder for less and less. If your dad could at least talk about the future of the place, admit that there are issues, then we might be able to get somewhere."

"Have you seen him yet?"

"No. He arrives tomorrow, but I'm not sure I want to see him right now. I just need some space. I can't believe he's left the Palace with only Grace in charge."

"Look, Mom. The last thing I need you to do right now is worry about the Palace. Before he left, Dad said that Grace has got everything under control with the weddings, and I'm going to stay here for a while as well. It's time Nick, Ari, and I stepped up a bit to help you out and that's what we'll do, so you've got nothing to worry about."

"But what about your thesis?" her mother said. "I don't want this affecting your studies."

"I've had a chat to my professor about the time I lost when I wasn't well and we both think it's best that I have a break and come back in the fall."

Her mother tilted her head on one side. "You promise me that decision's got nothing to do with me being away?"

Yasmin laughed. "Absolutely not. I'd made the decision on the plane on the way back. I'm actually really looking forward to spending some time in Brentwood Bay and catching up with some old friends."

"Well, don't you worry about me. When I've had a week or two of the Aegean sun and some good village meals, I'm sure I'll be starting to see things differently."

"And Nick and Ari? When are you going to tell them about the situation with you and dad?"

Pia rolled her lips together. "I'd rather not say anything about it in the meantime," she said. "To be honest I would rather your father hadn't said anything to you as well. You kids have got enough to worry about in your own lives without getting concerned about me and your dad."

So typical, Yasmin thought. Secrets and tiptoeing around issues was an Olympic sport in her family. Some days she'd trade anything for some brutal truth. Maybe that was something she could work on while she was here. Getting her family to be honest instead of treating each other like delicate strangers.

"Please at least see Dad while he's there," she said. "I know he can be infuriating, but what does it tell you that he's dropped everything here to come to you?"

"It tells me that he can't run that place without me and that he doesn't want the things that I want." Her mother shook her head. "Of course I'll talk to him. But I can't promise I can get him to listen."

"Enjoy your time there," Yasmin said. "Give everyone my love and please don't worry about anything. Everything will be just fine."

Yasmin ended the call and sat back in the chair. It broke her heart that her parents were going through such a tough time. They'd both worked hard her whole life and she wanted to help them out to solve some of their problems. She didn't have Nick's money, or Ari's brawn, but just maybe, with the help of Lane Griffiths, they could get the Palace to a point where business could be booming again, and maybe then her mom and dad would come home.

*Y*asmin sat in the apartment the next morning, thumbing the gold-edged piece of white card containing the bouquet list she'd written on the flight from Singapore. For something so significant, typing a list on her phone hadn't seemed quite right. It needed to be written out the old-fashioned way, with rich black ink in a loopy, flowing script. The card smelled like her grandmother's linen closet and she took an extra sniff. It was the scent of a bouquet, bright and positive and full of promise. Perfect.

She picked up the sleek black pen she'd bought with the card at a fancy stationery store in Singapore and put a tick beside the first three items on the list, and satisfaction flowed through her. She'd called her professor last night, and while he hadn't been happy with her decision to take a year's break from her PhD, he'd said he'd get in touch at the end of the semester and hoped she'd consider coming back then.

Her pen hovered above number four—learn a new language. She'd already downloaded a course in Italian onto her phone, but she wouldn't tick that entry until she could at least hold a brief conversation. In the cab from the airport she'd noticed a new pizza place that looked authentic. Maybe she could work up to ordering a full meal when she and Genie went out sometime.

Ten had seemed a nice round number for her list, but she'd come up with only nine so far. Something was sure to come to her, though, in the form of a crazy adventure sport to try, or a new way of dressing. She'd been experimenting with bright colors, but now with the purple streaks in her hair, she needed to think carefully about what clashed. Last night when Genie came over, she'd put on her favorite turquoise sweater and had ended up looking like some kind of disease molecule. Everything had always gone with black, so this would take thinking about.

Her gaze moved to number five and a thrill shot through her. *Seduce a man who's out of your league. Tall, dark, and mysterious. No chickening out!*

Tall, dark, mysterious—not to mention sexy as all get-out—Lane certainly fit the criteria for number five, but why not go after one of the Italian men in the pizza place? Well, for one, it made much more sense to try to seduce a man she had background information on. At least she knew Lane wasn't a serial killer. And besides, being her brother's best friend kinda made him even more out of her league, didn't it? And that would make the challenge of seducing him all the more authentic and satisfying.

The fact that never in her life had she tried to seduce anyone, especially someone like Lane, was the tiny matter she'd need to address. Genie had eagerly offered advice on her plan last night. Exploit plenty of tactile moments, she'd said—the hair touching, the gazing with deep and uninterrupted concentration whenever he talked, the hand brushing, the lip moistening. It had all become a jumble by the end of the night. Maybe she should write a list for that too?

Time to pull herself together. If she'd succumbed to the fear of getting a piercing or changing her hair color, she wouldn't have experienced the sense of lightness and freedom that doing something so un-Yasmin could give her. And she *did* feel great. Until a car door closed downstairs and butterflies took flight in her belly.

She checked out the window for the hundredth time that morning, and sure enough it was Lane. He drove a late-model European car. An Aston Martin? A Mercedes? She wasn't sure, but it was sleek and silver, and as he unfolded his frame from the driver's seat and did up the button on his jacket, she found a little more resolve to follow through with her plan. He was even more gorgeous than the million memories she had of him from yesterday.

His suit was different today though; this one was inky blue and the shirt collar beneath it was cream. It set the light tan of his skin off so beautifully she couldn't help wondering what he'd look like in something more casual, a T-shirt and jeans for example. Or maybe a tank top and shorts—an outfit that showed more of the fine muscles she just knew lay beneath that business look. He ran his fingers through his dark hair, and it stayed in exactly the same perfect style. No, she couldn't imagine Lane Griffiths ever wearing a tank top and board shorts. His pajamas probably came as a three-piece suit with a built-in tie. She swallowed as she imagined Lane in pajamas. And then not in pajamas, or anything else ...

The doorbell chimed and she shook herself from her X-rated thoughts. She quickly blew on the ink to make sure it was dry, popped the card back in its little plastic sleeve, then raced down the stairs.

"Good morning," she said when she pulled the door open. "I'm glad you knew to come to the apartment instead of the house. I forgot to tell you I was staying here."

"I've been here a few times since your parents moved," he said. "I'm sorry I'm a little early." He looked down as he wiped his feet. "I'm finding the lack of a job a bit of a challenge."

He'd been back regularly? "No problem." She stood aside and let him pass. The fact he'd still get dressed up without an office to go to—and that it was the weekend— was super cute. She thought of the way she'd felt when she'd woken without an alarm this morning. No textbooks on her nightstand, no thesis deadline to meet. The only thing she'd felt was excitement that she was going to get reacquainted with Lane, and this time he wasn't going to have a choice but to notice her.

She took a deeper breath as his scent drifted past, a delicious soap-and-freshly-shaved aroma that she'd be happy to breathe all day.

"I was always in the restaurant or behind my desk at seven thirty, so all this time on my hands makes me a bit antsy." He turned to her and their eyes met. His lips tilted in a sexy smile. Warmth prickled across the back of her neck, and her mouth became dry at the thought of what she'd vowed for herself this morning.

She *could* seduce a man like Lane Griffiths. Of course she could. They were both young and, she desperately hoped, unattached; it was summer, and they had an excuse to spend a whole lot of time together. But did he even find her attractive? There'd been the comment about her hair yesterday, and she thought she'd caught him checking her out while she was eating that scone, but then he'd poured cold water on all her ideas—maybe he saw her as a pain in the butt?

As he moved through the hallway, she realized they were both in a bit of a transition phase: he'd sold his businesses and she'd decided to turn her life upside down. She didn't think she'd ever have the problem of needing to get to work early, though.

"My uncle Leo, our chef, won't be in the kitchen for another hour. He won an award at a culinary thing last night for a side business he has, so I told him to come in late. I can show you around the restaurant first if you like. Or would you rather have a coffee?"

"If there's a wait, a coffee would be good."

The thought of being alone with him, chatting about their next few weeks together, almost caused her to lose her nerve. *No chickening out!* "Just go to the top of the stairs."

He started up the stairs in front of her, back straight, body in perfect alignment.

Despite the fact that she'd known him for years, there was still this formality between them, as if he had a barrier around himself. For the first time, she registered that he was holding a briefcase. Did people still do that? On a Sunday? With the ability to carry documents on laptops and smart-phones, what was the point? She couldn't help but wonder what he had hidden inside there.

"The Palace hasn't changed much at all," he said. "Your parents have invited me to every Easter Sunday lunch since I was about ten."

He reached the top and she moved in front of him to the kitchen. "I guess that's part of the whole problem with the Palace. Mom and Dad haven't had the energy or direction— or the money, I guess—to change things up."

Lane perched on a stool at the counter and picked up an

empty Pop-Tart packet as if it were a dead mouse. "Breakfast?"

She leaned forward and grabbed it from him. "That's all there was in the cupboard."

One dark eyebrow rose slowly, and his eyes sparkled. She swallowed. "You'll need your strength if you intend to be completely involved in this renovation."

"There's a lot of strength in a Pop-Tart," she said, stuffing the wrapper into the trash to avoid his gaze. She reminded herself not to tell him about being sick. She didn't need him any more dubious about her abilities than he already was. "Leo will make us something nice for lunch, I'm sure."

He patted his briefcase. "It's okay. I have a packed lunch."

So that's what was in there. She could imagine he'd carefully made sandwiches, ensuring all the nutritional groups were represented, and that they were cut in equilateral triangles. "I bet you make a good one."

"I don't have time to make my own normally," he said dismissively. "I have a regular order with my local Sandwich Sensation, and they have it waiting for me each morning."

She gaped at him. "You mean you have the same thing for lunch every day?"

He scoffed. "Of course not. Sunday is turkey day."

"Then what do you have on the real Turkey Day?"

There was a pause. "Sandwich Sensation is closed, so I get lunch from one of my restaurants."

She turned around and took two cups from a high cupboard and allowed herself a quick grin while she was at it. Just as well he was so irresistible, or his straitlaced routine might start to put her off.

Tring! The mindfulness bell on her phone went off, and its long, musical note floated around the room. She certainly didn't need reminding to be in the moment right now. She was having no problems focusing on the man in front of her.

"That's an interesting ringtone," he said, frowning. "Sounds like a particularly annoying doorbell."

She just smiled, certain that the idea of mindfulness would seem kooky to a man like Lane.

"What were you doing overseas, exactly?" he asked as she turned back to him.

She took the carafe of coffee and poured a mug for him, and waited while water boiled for her tea. "I was doing research for my PhD—studying nitrogen nutrition and isotopic discrimination in ectomycorrhizal fungi, to be precise."

He didn't bat an eyelid. "Fungi?"

"Mushrooms, toadstools, truffles. They all have their charms."

"Do you have a favorite?"

"*Laccaria amethystina*, the amethyst deceiver."

He lifted the mug and grinned. "Sounds like some sort of sneaky assassin."

She laughed. "It's not quite that exciting, but it kinda grows on you—if you'll excuse the fungi pun. Mycologists get a bit of a bad rap for having no sense of humor, but you can always make jokes about being a 'fun guy' or whether there's 'mush room' in here."

Lane looked at her deadpan. "No shiitake."

She laughed out loud. Was that the first even slightly amusing thing he'd said since yesterday? Was there actually a funny bone within that body full of self-confident aloofness?

She tipped her mug at him. "You're good."

The eyebrow again. "I know."

The air sizzled and she absently put the mug to her lips before she realized it was empty.

"I'm glad to hear you're still studying. After I saw you, I mean at the ... when we met again yesterday, you weren't how I remembered."

"I'm taking time out from my PhD, and do you mean I was dull and conservative before?"

"I don't remember you being dull, but yes, I do remember you wearing coveralls and glasses that gave the impression you were doing some spot-welding," he said in a teasing voice.

"I'm still as blind as a bat; I just wear ten-inch-thick contacts now." She squinted at him for effect and then poured water onto her tea bag. "We can take these out into the courtyard if you like."

"Sure."

"Do you live close by?" she asked when they were downstairs and walking through the corridor that led out into the restaurant courtyard. There wasn't a wedding today, so everything was quiet. "I remember you lived over on Robinson Street. Are your parents still there?" As soon as she'd said it, she wished the ground would open up and swallow her. He'd always had two homes, one on Robinson and the other on Green, and he'd spent as much time at the Palace as he could to avoid each of them.

"My mother still lives on Robinson, but my father lives in the city now. The newest Prescott Hotel's in San Francisco, so I'll move back when we've finished here. I'll be living and breathing my new restaurant come December and I won't want any distractions."

They'd stepped into the courtyard, the sun glaring bright as it reflected off the whitewashed walls of the restaurant. Brilliant magenta bougainvillea cascaded down at intervals and, as she did every time she entered this court-yard, Yasmin felt like a breath of fresh air had been blown across her soul.

A loud noise came from the corner of the courtyard. "That's gotta be Monty."

Yasmin turned to him and smiled. "Yep, he's fifteen now, and still as cheeky as ever. He swears in about ten different languages, I think." They walked over to the parrot's huge cage and Yasmin realized what had set him off. The fluffy black and white cat who'd greeted her yesterday was sitting in a patch of sun, his head on one side as if mocking the parrot.

"You must be Boris," Yasmin said as she bent to pat the cat. He looked up at her and then continued looking at Monty. "Apparently Boris is staying while my cousin and his girlfriend are overseas," she said to Lane. "I don't think Monty's a fan."

She stood and reached into her pocket for a peanut. Monty bounced up and down on the perch he was sitting on and nodded his head.

"Hey, Monty." Lane's rich voice was deeper than ever as he peered into the cage and talked quietly to the bird. He put his briefcase down and leaned closer. "No, I'm not going to put my fingers through the bars because I remember you can be a cantankerous old buzzard."

"I'm going to strangle that bird's neck, strangle that bird's neck!" Monty squawked. "Mano, I'll strangle that bird's neck!"

"That's my mom's voice." Yasmin laughed. "Can you hear his Greek accent? Every time Mom hears Monty cuss, she says she'll wring his neck, but she loves him more than anyone."

Lane pushed both hands into his trouser pockets and

gave her a serious look. "How do you think things are with your parents?"

Yasmin held one of the bars of Monty's cage. "I don't really know. They've always tried to keep any tension between the two of them secret from us, so I never know what's the truth. I FaceTimed Mom last night and she wasn't her usual self. I think she's exhausted from working so hard here."

"Morning." They both turned to see Grace Bennett, the Palace's wedding planner, smiling as she walked past in a powder-blue suit.

"Oh, Grace, this is Lane Griffiths. He's come to advise on the changes to the restaurant. Lane, this is our incredible wedding planner, Grace. Here on a Sunday. We're so lucky to have her. She works crazy hours."

"Nice to meet you, Lane." Grace held out her hand and Boris pressed against her ankles. "No wedding today, so I can catch up a bit. Mano mentioned you'd be around while he and Pia are away. I'm really looking forward to your ideas for the Palace. I've always loved your restaurants and can't wait 'til your new place is open."

Lane shook her hand, and they had a brief conversation about people they both knew, the fortunes of the wedding business, and how wonderful Lane's new hotel restaurant would be. Suddenly, it struck Yasmin that Grace was probably the sort of girl Lane usually dated. Well-groomed and well-connected, confident but singularly business minded. She was the sort of dependable and consistent woman Lane would be instantly attracted to. And he wouldn't be out of her league at all.

"I'd appreciate you being involved in our decisions here, Grace," Lane was saying. "After all, you're the one who'll have to make everything work."

"I'll look forward to it," she said. "Excuse me for now, though. I have an important flower plan to check on for tomorrow. Come with me, Boris. I see that Leo's put some food in your bowl."

As Grace entered the office building and closed the door behind them, Lane turned to her. "Your dad says she does a great job here."

"Yes, she's amazing. We'd be completely lost without her. She's been here for about five years and manages all the day-to-day running of the wedding business now."

He nodded. "I'm taking all my best staff with me to the hotel. Good people are worth their weight in gold. I guess there are a few employees who'll be worried that your parents aren't here."

Did he mean that they must be worried that she was in charge when she really knew nothing about this business at all?

"I guess. Grace is very aware of what's happening, and Leo is family. Most of the others don't know the full story yet, just that Dad's gone to Greece to bring Mom home. I don't want to tell them anything else just now so that we can keep things as stable as possible. Dad said he'd rather Nick didn't know the whole story right now, either, so if you wouldn't mind ..."

Lane set his hands low on his hips. "No problem. And it's best the employees are told the bare minimum. The last thing we need is staff deserting us or spreading any rumors about there being issues. When people are shelling out the sort of money they do for a wedding, they wouldn't want any hint that things weren't going to be absolutely perfect and uninterrupted."

Yasmin fingered the butterfly at her throat. "I really want to make a difference here, Lane. I'm not just doing this to kill time, or because I think it's going to be a fun thing to have on my CV. I'm really committed to helping Mom and Dad put things back on track."

"I'm glad to hear it," he said as he picked his briefcase up again. "While I know plenty about what it takes to run a good restaurant, and you've grown up in this place, I don't think either of us has a complete enough knowledge about the way a successful wedding hall should work, so we're going to need to utilize the expertise of people like Grace."

As times had gotten tougher in the wedding business, her parents had decided to open it to the public when there wasn't a wedding on—which was quite often these days. Her uncle Leo was an incredible chef but had always deferred to her parents' taste and style, and she was hoping that part of the changes they'd make would be to update the menu.

"Is here okay?" Yasmin indicated a couple of chairs and they both sat. "Leo shouldn't be too far away."

Lane put the briefcase and his coffee mug on the table, flicked the case open, and pulled out three glossy brochures. "As I was saying, we'll need to talk to Grace and all the key staff here before we make any changes, as our decisions will affect them, but it would make sense to try to work out what other wedding halls are doing that you aren't. Here are three brochures from your competitors."

Yasmin picked up one of the glossy documents and flicked through the pictures of beautiful brides and perfect table settings. "Yes, Patterson Weddings, for example. That place has been Mom and Dad's direct competition for years, and while things have been getting harder and harder here, they've recently expanded, and I've heard they're fully booked for two years. It would be great to find out how they do it."

"Yes, but you can bet the Pattersons aren't going to give

up their secrets that easily. I know there's been a feud between your families for years. By the way, how did it start?"

Yasmin sighed. "Apparently there was a big society wedding they were both hoping to get but the Pattersons won. Dad said they cheated, but who knows."

"If we want to find out why the Pattersons are so successful, we'll need to try to find people to talk to about their experiences there, or maybe get some video footage inside during a wedding."

A clear and perfectly formed idea slunk its way into Yasmin's head. Something that could help in the renovation and guarantee her some time away from the Palace with Lane. "What if we went as guests? I've been invited to my friend Paul's wedding there the weekend after next. The bride's mother is friends with Mrs. Patterson. You could come as my date, and we could treat it like an undercover investigation."

"They'll recognize you, of course," he said, with the inscrutable gaze that made the skin at the back of her neck heat.

"If Mr. and Mrs. Patterson are there they might, but I'd imagine they mostly have managers running things. And if any of the other family members see us there it'll be too late to change or hide anything. What do you say?"

He scrubbed his hand across his chin. "Maybe."

Lane as her date at a wedding, where she'd have the chance to get dressed up, and possibly even dance with him? She shivered a little with excitement. Maybe the seduction of Lane Griffiths had a chance after all. But that was more than a week away, and she couldn't wait that long. "Of course they're not going to have the Greek choices on their menu that we have here, so I also think it's important for us to visit some contemporary Greek restaurants."

He nodded. "There's a good one near me, Constantino's Cuizina."

"How about we go there tomorrow night?" She felt a little light-headed as all the possible ways she could get closer to him materialized. She might not have him hooked yet, but at least they were heading in the right direction now, and when the time was right she'd reel him in.

He shook his head. "I'm sorry, I can't tomorrow night. I have an appointment."

An appointment, or a date? Suddenly, stage one in her plan to seduce Lane Griffiths began to unravel in front of her.

"Oh, I'm sorry." Yasmin's face slackened and she twirled a piece of her Day-Glo hair between her fingers. "Here's me inviting you out for dinner and attempting to commandeer your weekend, and your whole life for the next month, without considering what else you might have going on." She bit her lip and looked at him with those big brown eyes … as though he'd asked her out and then decided he had something better to do.

"No problem." He pulled his phone from his pocket and flicked to the calendar so she'd think he could keep his eyes off her. Even though he couldn't. He was pretty sure tomorrow night's meeting was the only thing he had all week, but Yasmin didn't need to know that. "How about tonight?"

The rose tint that he'd seen yesterday crawled up her neck, and Yasmin waved the air with her hand. He'd never considered that a blush could be so sexy until he'd seen one on Yasmin. "No, I was just getting carried away. You're the restaurant professional. I'm sure you know enough about Greek food already, or else you can talk to your friends about it." She picked up another of the brochures and flipped through it. "And I'm going to Paul's wedding anyway, there's no reason you have to come with me to that."

Surprised by the hurt tone in her voice, he stopped scrolling through the calendar and looked at her. "Actually, I don't know a lot about Greek food—apart from your mom's cooking. Hers was the only home-cooked food I had when I was young. My mother always took me out for dinner after she left my father, and Dad was clueless about cooking, so when I was with him we lived off takeout."

Yasmin tipped her head to one side and frowned. "Then how on earth did you get into the restaurant business? I just pictured all restaurateurs having grown up with good food and home cooking."

"When I was sixteen, I'd gotten sick of the to-ing and fro-ing between my parents, and I wanted to avoid it all, so I started washing dishes in a local restaurant. I'd known from watching your parents that running a food joint took a lot of time and energy, but I also liked being around lots of people all the time. I never had that at home."

"Things must have been hard for you."

Her eyes had softened, and he cleared his throat, not wanting to go down that road with her. Or anyone. "I think you're right," he said as he went back to looking at his calendar. "We should take a look at some fresh ideas, and tonight works for me. We don't have a lot of time for this. I only have a month until construction begins on my new restaurant complex, so the sooner we get on it the better."

"Then you could go with Leo. He'll need to be involved

with the changes to the menu," she said, as if she was having second thoughts about spending time with him.

He rubbed his hand at the back of his neck. A minute ago she was excited and making constructive plans about how they should tackle this, and now she was backing off. Maybe he'd given her the impression that he didn't take her or this project seriously enough. It was true that his project in San Francisco was his lifelong dream—being the best of the best and being in charge of his own destiny. He wouldn't let anything get in the way of achieving that, but he wanted her to know what this renovation meant to him, too.

"I always loved sitting around your family's dinner table." And he didn't mean Pia's perfect cheese pies, or the desserts running with honey and nuts; he meant the warmth and the noise, and the good-humored banter that he still looked forward to every time he visited here. "I used to dream about your noisy family dinners and the way every problem could be solved by a good meal." He had a clearer memory of her as a kid now; she always seemed kind of shy when she was around him and Nick, but with her whole family, she was just as loud and confident as they were. "So, I'm off to dinner with Leo?"

Her face fell and she held her hands out. "Actually, no, I've just remembered, Leo *can't* go with you tonight. Because of the award for his bread business, Grace is hoping for extra bookings in the restaurant, so she'll want him to be here."

Lane nodded. "Then it'll just be you and me. Eating a whole pile of dolmas and coming up with our plan."

∼

43

Lane checked his messages while he waited in his car for Yasmin to come downstairs early that evening. He wasn't quite sure how he'd been roped into being with her around food again—watching her savor a whole three courses could be dangerous to his health. He was gambling his survival on the fact that a Greek restaurant wouldn't serve whipped cream.

She'd tried to convince him to meet her at Constantino's, but he'd been around the Katsalos family long enough to know what were the right and wrong ways to call on a woman, whether it was a business meeting or not, and she'd agreed to his waiting outside. Treating a woman with respect had been one of Mano's mantras.

He'd learned way more about those sorts of life lessons from Mano Katsalos than he had from his own father. His dad was more interested in scoring points from his mom as they passed him back and forth from week to week. They'd split when he was two, so he had no real memory of happy family times until he'd met Nick and been welcomed into his family. Of course, his future would be filled with many happy times now, running his own restaurant in the most modern hotel in the world. He'd create his own memories from now on.

Hearing a door shut, he looked up through the windshield. As soon as he saw Yasmin walking toward him, his breathing stopped. She looked like a style icon from a midcentury movie, all color and shine and heart-seizing beauty. He got out of the car and went to open the door for her, still watching her every move.

She was wearing the most shockingly green dress he'd ever seen. It was an Amy Winehouse 1950s sort of thing, with a tight waist and a flared skirt, and it absolutely, 100 percent clashed with the purple of her hair. Enormous hoop earrings swayed against her neck as she walked. The look on her face suggested she didn't give a damn about anything, a grin stretching from ear to ear.

"Thanks," she said as she slid into the passenger seat before he moved around to the driver's side.

"So is this the way you treat all your dates?" She grinned as he got in. "Opening doors like an old movie star?"

While this might look like a date—and the feeling when he'd first seen her might make it feel like one—they both needed to remember that it was anything but. "Only the ones with fathers who would line me up against a wall and shoot me if I didn't treat their little girls right." He started the engine and pulled out into the street.

"But Dad is miles across the Atlantic," Yasmin said. "I'm going to pretend you did it because that's the way you always like to treat a girl." She brushed the fabric of the skirt across her knees. "I'm glad we could do this tonight; on account of the date you have tomorrow."

"Yes, it worked out well." He wasn't sure what had given her the idea his meeting tomorrow was a date. "What sort of things were you hoping to look at tonight?"

She frowned, then shifted on her seat. "I'm hoping we'll get inspiration for new things to put on the menu, but I also want to get new ideas for decor. We don't want to change the special Greek atmosphere of the Palace's restaurant, but there must be ways to make it more fresh."

"I agree. According to my research, there are still plenty of families who hold on to their Greek traditions but who aren't having their weddings at the Palace. Why do you think that is?"

Yasmin shrugged and the puffy sleeve of her dress slipped a little, baring a shoulder, and he imagined reaching over and touching her smooth skin.

"I don't know. I suspect it's because Mom and Dad haven't moved with the times," she said, oblivious to his distraction. "The first- and second-generation kids still want to hold on to some of the old traditions, but they want to incorporate American things too. I think if we can get a balance, we'll be on the right track."

"What would you want to have for your wedding?"

She turned to him and tucked a piece of hair behind her ear. "Me?" She laughed, a light and sweet sound. "A wedding? That's one thing I'm not planning on. Ever."

"Really? Why not?"

"I guess it feels like another expectation for me, like something I'm *supposed* to do. Even if I did decide to have a ceremony, I couldn't imagine that he'd be a Greek guy, so a wedding in a flashy place like the Palace wouldn't suit me. I'm planning on meeting a guy on a beach on the other side of the world and just going where the mood takes us."

He couldn't stop himself from frowning, still trying to reconcile the image he'd always had of Yasmin with the colorful creature sitting in his coupe. Her sexiness had shocked him when they'd met in the tea shop, but now he was more intrigued by the fact that he still felt that way about her when they were clearly so different.

"How about you?" Her voice softened. "Are you after the big wedding?"

His fingers curled around the steering wheel. "Absolutely. But I have no illusions. Finding the right person will take time and consideration. I guess it's like my new restaurant—it's something I've always aspired to, and when the time was right I made it happen. When I do find her, I want a marriage that I can be proud of, a relationship that's alive and evolving." Before she could ask him any more he said, "I reckon Nick will want to have a traditional wedding too."

"Ooooh, yes. Nick will want to have the expensive white wedding and the wife who does what he tells her to. She'll be from the right sort of family and know that she's never quite going to be his equal. He and Dad have always thought that women were a little hopeless."

"That's a bit harsh."

She looked out her side window and smoothed the fabric of her skirt. "They can be a bit Neanderthal at times."

"I think they both care a lot about you." Lane slowed for a red light and turned to her. "There's a lot worse you could have in your life than people who are looking out for you."

"Of course."

"When are you going to tell Nick about what's happening with your parents?"

She shrugged. "I'll let them decide that. I think Dad's hoping he'll have Mom back here by the end of the week and that Nick and Ari will be none the wiser, but I don't like secrets. I tried to FaceTime Mom after you left this morning, but she wasn't at my aunt's. I'll call her tomorrow, see if she's caught up with Dad yet and find out what she's going to tell my brothers. Hey, look," she said, pointing out the window. "You and Nick used to do karate in that old building, didn't you?"

"You remember that?"

"Of course. I used to come watch you sometimes."

He sensed she didn't want to talk about her family anymore, so he turned the conversation back to the restaurant. "We'll need to win a whole new crowd who want something more contemporary and a little bit European in our redesign. Have you been to Constantino's?"

Her shoulders relaxed and she stopped stroking the fabric of her dress. "No, but I've heard of him. I haven't been home much since I moved to New York for college."

"I let Constantino know we were coming. I've done advisory work for him in the past, so I asked if he could be there tonight for a quick chat after we've eaten, and he agreed."

"Have you been seeing her for a while?"

Lane frowned, unsure whom Yasmin was talking about. "Sorry, who?"

She'd started the fabric-stroking thing again and he sat forward in his seat. Behind that newly confident exterior there were still hints of the reserved girl he'd known, and he couldn't figure her out. He stopped at a red light. His old high school was on the corner, and he tried to think back to what Yasmin was like when they were younger. Why were his memories of her so vague?

"The girl tomorrow."

"Oh, Lisa. We meet regularly. I have a charity organization in the city that picks up leftover food from supermarkets and restaurants and delivers it to soup kitchens. She coordinates the work, and we catch up from time to time about it. Chances are we'll spend most of the evening talking about that. Why?"

"Oh, no reason." She still looked nervous, smoothing her dress and looking out the window. "I was just wondering if she'd be okay with us going to the wedding together. You spending a whole day with another woman."

"It's not a date, and most people who know me understand that work's the most important thing in my life. Besides, you're my best friend's little sister. What could anyone be worried about?"

He looked across at her and the tiniest of smiles curved her mouth. Each time she stroked the skirt of her dress, his pulse gave an extra beat and his grip on the steering wheel tightened. What would it be like to be the one stroking that thigh? Kissing the smile on those lips?

Abruptly, he turned his attention back to the windshield and focused on the road in front. Those were questions he'd never know the answer to, and must never attempt to find out.

∽

What could anyone be worried about? That he might reject you? Or laugh in your face, or wonder why someone like you could ever imagine he'd be interested ...

Yasmin turned her head slightly so she could see Lane as he concentrated on the road. He was such a man. A responsible and capable man, with a busy life and goals and dreams of big business. If even he believed he was out of her league, then that just proved he was perfect for number five on her list. But how in the name of all good things did you go about seducing your older brother's best friend? Or any guy that you'd only ever admired from afar, and only imagined talking to in your dreams?

Going from high school to college and then graduate school had meant that dating was always low on her list of things to focus on. Of course she'd had boyfriends before, but they'd been like her, geeky studious types who were more interested in science projects during the week and house parties at the weekend.

While they drove, Lane talked about things he and Nick had got up to when they were younger, and she sat wondering how she was going to seduce him at the restaurant when they were supposed to be talking business.

Did you start by removing your shoe and slowly rubbing his leg under the table with your toes? She'd seen that in a movie once and the guy had thought there was a spider crawling up his leg, leaped up, and spilled a bowl of minestrone all down his white pants. She couldn't imagine Lane ever wearing white pants, so maybe she could try that.

Perhaps she could mention she'd been thinking about how hard his pecs might be when she passed him the butter. She suppressed a cough. Truth be told, she couldn't imagine saying something like that without her face getting so red it burst into flames.

As they got closer to the restaurant, her stomach began to twist tighter and tighter. Talking about when they were young made her remember that feeling of being invisible, as though Lane could only ever see straight through her. What was she going to do now that would make him start to really notice her?

4

Sitting at a corner table in Constantino's Greek restaurant while Lane talked about profit margins on entrées and the finer points of a good dessert, all Yasmin could do was watch the way his strong jaw moved and the way his eyes lit up when he talked about his businesses.

That he was the perfect candidate for number five on her list wasn't an issue; the question was more about whether he'd be into a casual relationship for fun and mutual satisfaction, and whether he even found her attractive. There was no getting Dutch courage from a glass of wine or two; her damaged liver from the dengue fever had made sure of that. She took a sip of her sparkling water.

Of course she could just wait and see if anything developed between them, but that would be living by her old rules. Her life from now on was about taking each day by the scruff of its neck and shaking it until she got what she wanted. And what she wanted was Lane's strong arms wrapped around her.

The problem was that everything she'd done so far to flirt with him had been an abysmal failure. She'd twirled her hair and he'd wondered if that was a good idea given the trauma it had gone through with the coloring. She'd rested her chin on her hands and looked at him while he'd talked, and he'd said her octopus would get cold. He'd commented on the brightness of her dress, mentioned numerous embarrassing incidents from when they were growing up, and given a confused sort of smile when she said that they had a lot in common these days.

He didn't smile much, but when he did, it was as if he'd been considering whether the moment was worthy enough to bestow one of his warm grins on it, and it sent little fingers of light through her body. But his aloofness was a big part of his charm, and a part of the challenge. There must be a way to burrow under that thick skin, a way to find a relaxed and fun-loving Lane within the buttoned-down exterior. The trick would be to work out a way to release him, and perhaps the buttons on that shirt he was wearing. There was no time like the present.

"Do you think I've changed?" She was interrupting his list of possible new menu choices, but if this seduction ball wasn't rolling soon it might never happen.

He looked up, his fork poised in midair, and his eyes sparked. "Of course. The braids you had when you were ten weren't purple." He stabbed at something on the plate in front of him and held it up. "You haven't tried this squid yet. The way they've braised it with currants and red wine is unusual, but it works. It's probably not a great choice for a wedding, but it'd be a nice appetizer on the regular restaurant menu."

"Have I changed in a good way or a bad?"

"Good, of course," he said and continued chewing, but he frowned. "But I thought you were fine before."

Fine? God, she really wasn't good at this.

He pointed with his fork to the walls and furniture, completely oblivious to the first of her seduction techniques. "How do you think this decor works? I like the turquoise and silver color scheme to represent the colors of Greece, but I'd probably make it even more contemporary—use more glass and brushed metal, but with the budget—"

"I didn't realize you'd noticed me before." She did the slow blink thing that Genie had insisted would be guaranteed to get his attention. It felt like she was one of those openmouthed clowns at the fair, waiting for him to put a ping-pong ball in her mouth.

There was that warm grin again. It was small and hard won, but man, it was worth the wait. "I noticed you when you followed Nick and me around, wanting to know how our toy guns worked, pleading with us to help you with one of your experiments."

She took another mouthful of the water and let her shoulders relax as the bubbles tickled the roof of her mouth. He'd been surprised when she said she wouldn't have a glass of wine. She'd thought about disclosing her illness, but she still wasn't sure that he wouldn't tell her parents how bad things had been, or worse, stop her from being involved at all.

"I noticed you all the time." There, she'd said it. She held her breath.

"Why, because you were wondering if I'd try to put a frog down your back?"

She didn't answer, just stared at him the way Genie had promised would have him begging for her to touch him. He looked up and the expression on his face changed and he gave a small cough. "Don't tell me you had a *crush* on me."

Was his emphasis on "crush" because he was completely horrified by the concept, or because he'd been hoping for so long that she'd felt that way that he couldn't believe she'd finally said it? She had a nasty feeling it was the first choice. And what a horrible word "crush" was anyway, sort of immature and desperate. Is that the way she was behaving now? Suddenly she felt very tired, and the warning her doctor had given her to take things easy these next few weeks rang in her head. But she'd started this now ...

The familiar sound of her mindfulness bell in her bag punctuated the air between them.

No chickening out.

"Of course I had a crush on you. You must've known that."

He chuckled, and when she didn't respond, the smile slipped from his face.

"I still do."

He stopped chewing but didn't say anything. Then he swallowed and his face became even more serious.

She placed the knife and fork beside her plate and forced words beyond the band tightening around her throat. "I had a wake-up call in Borneo. Being so far away from home made me reassess things."

"In what way?"

"I've always been a careful person, Lane, someone who'll weigh up the odds and always go with the completely safe bet—I guess it's the scientist in me—but I was denying myself a whole lot of life experiences. Since I was challenged overseas, faced difficult times, then overcame them, I realized I had the power to live my own life."

He was nodding slowly. "The purple hair. Taking time off your studies. You're trying something new."

He smiled as if he completely understood what she meant, and the positive tone to his voice made her heart skip.

"Yes, and the nose stud, and a whole lot of other things that I've always been too careful to try. I've made a list of everything I've promised to do for myself, and you're on there too."

He put down his fork and tried to hide his shock at what she'd just said. "You mean working with me on the restaurant renovation? I thought you only decided to do it when your mother went back to Greece."

She took another drink, but a rose tint blossomed on her cheeks and it was all at once sexy and sweet. "No, I mean seducing you. *That* was on my list."

He stopped moving ... and blinking. In fact, he had to remind himself to take another breath.

Her dark brown eyes were fixed on him. "Oh." He put his fork on the plate and then carefully lined it up with his knife. "That's not what I was expecting."

"Because you don't find me attractive?"

"Well, no, I mean yes, it's ..." He cleared his throat. He couldn't tell her how he'd felt that first time he saw her again, or what it was like sitting here with her now with her fresh face and her aura of fun. "We haven't seen each other in years, Yasmin. I only really remember you as a little kid, and now your dad's ... Your father has asked me to be his project manager for this. He told me to keep ..."

She spoke more forcefully. "Dad told you to keep what?"

He picked up his napkin, wiped his hands, then put it down again. "Your dad called me from the airport and asked me to keep an eye on you while he and your mother weren't here."

Yasmin sighed hard and rolled her eyes to the ceiling. "I

guess looking after myself for the last five years, working halfway across the world, and being self-sufficient and successful all happened by accident."

He rested his arms on the table. "Should I be worried about this list? That you're going to start doing a whole lot of things that are out of character?" The glow on her cheeks suggested that's exactly what she'd do.

"The things I want to do now aren't out of character for me, they're simply not what people expect. If I hadn't made the commitment to go after the things I really wanted in my life, then I wouldn't have dreamed of saying these things. I wouldn't have had the courage. But the fact is I don't want to live that way anymore." She laid both palms flat on the table. "Lane, I'm going to do what I want rather than what's expected of me from now on, go after the things I didn't have the confidence to ask for. That includes you."

Lane kept his eyes fixed on Yasmin's face. Listening to her explain in well-thought-out and logical detail why he should let himself be seduced by her would've had any other guy in this room on the edge of his seat, or halfway out the door with her hand in his. She was beautiful and intelligent, and had a laugh that made people turn around and smile. But he wasn't a regular guy, and the sooner she understood that, the better.

For one thing, he didn't want a relationship with anyone right now. He was about to build a brand-new restaurant in one of the most prestigious hotel chains in the world, he kept antisocial hours, and he didn't need any distractions.

Not only that, when there had been no one else to turn to as a kid, when Lane had been traded back and forth between his parents like a bad debt, he'd come to understand that you made only a few real friends like Nick Katsalos in your life. To say that Nick had saved his sanity when they were growing up might sound like the script from a soap opera, but it was true. Lane would do anything for Nick and his family. And he would never, ever hurt them.

Lane was the guy who'd been charged by Mano Katsalos to keep an eye on his daughter until he got back. Mano was his best friend's father, and you did what he asked. It was one thing to disappoint a girl whose family he didn't know, but when any relationship he might have with Yasmin broke down, as it surely would given how different they were, she'd still have her family, but he wouldn't. And he couldn't risk that happening.

Yasmin was sitting across from him, her face flushed, and her fingers knitted together in front of her as if she was waiting for him to pass down a sentence. Her hair was pulled off her face and the tiny diamond in her nose twinkled under the restaurant lights.

"Yasmin, I ..."

"I've embarrassed you, haven't I?" She gave him a rueful smile. "Well, join the club, but I won't apologize for going after something that I want, and I'm not changing my mind. I'm not unattractive, you and I have had some great laughs together, and we're both going to be moving along in a few weeks, so what have we got to lose?"

He scratched his head, as if putting his hand a little closer to his brain might give him some inspiration for getting out of this without hurting her feelings. Not unattractive? That was the understatement of the year. Yasmin had always been striking with her long black hair and her high Grecian cheekbones, but now, with her new hair color and the out-there way she was dressing, she was the sort of person you'd crane your neck to get another look at. What could a woman like her see in someone as focused and predictable as him?

"Yasmin, I'm flattered, I really am. But I've promised your dad we'll have an updated restaurant opening a month from now. That's my priority." He shifted the napkin from one side of his plate to the other. "You don't really want a guy like me. Look at you. You should be with some artsy type, a poet or an architect at least. Someone who likes socializing. And I'm none of those things."

She touched the delicate butterfly at her neck. Damn if it wasn't one of the sexiest things about her. A headache bit behind his eyes. Was he mad? Had the grinding hours of work and the lonely road of being in charge and making money fried every cell in his brain?

She lifted a slim shoulder and her eyes twinkled. "Well, I guess you can't blame a girl for trying."

"Dessert? We have pistachio ice cream or a delicious cardamom cream pie."

Oh God, not more whipped cream!

The waiter stood in front of them and a smile slowly spread across Yasmin's face. She looked back at Lane, and he'd never wished so hard that he could be someone completely different, someone who could live life on a whim like she obviously could. But whims were transitory and fleeting, and that wasn't the way he wanted to live his life, or the way he'd treat relationships.

"Well, the least you can do is be a gentleman and share a piece of cream pie."

He looked into her eyes and wondered, now that he knew what she wanted from him, how he could keep away from her for a month.

Yasmin sat in the Palace restaurant the next day, waiting for Lane to appear. She'd been making notes on her laptop getting ready for their meeting this morning, but now she stared at the screen as her thoughts wandered to last night.

What a complete and absolute embarrassment she'd been to herself. Why had she intellectualized it all and tried to explain what she wanted? If she'd just done what most normal people do—find the right moment, then make a move—things might've turned out differently. She picked up the remains of her breakfast, a piece of Leo's warm olive bread, and chewed. And if Lane hadn't been such a gentleman and tried to change the subject after she'd embarrassed him beyond belief, she quite likely wouldn't have come out from under her rock this morning.

They'd ended the night with him dropping her home, and she'd apologized for making him feel weird about her proposition but told him she was glad she'd said it. He'd just smiled and said that he'd forget all about it.

She brushed crumbs from her orange silk batwing top. *Get your act together.* Feeling sorry and embarrassed wouldn't cut the mustard anymore. If her hair hadn't turned out, she'd have just tried again, wouldn't she? If her nose stud wasn't quite right, she'd fix it. Just because her first choice of tall, dark, and way-out-of-her-league didn't want her for now, then she'd either have to keep on trying, or find someone who would. In the meantime she had her Italian lesson app on her phone and was doing an hour's practice every morning.

Suddenly, the FaceTime alert jumped on her laptop screen. Her mom was calling from Greece. They'd arranged to speak at noon, time for her meeting with Lane this morning to be over. Should she answer it or just let it ring? The thought of her mother sitting nervously in front of a borrowed computer, maybe desperate to talk, was too much to bear and she clicked to make the connection.

"Hey, Mom. How are you?"

"Great, now that I can see you. Is now a good time?"

"Actually, I have a meeting with Lane in a minute. Can I call you back later?"

"Ah, Lane. He's such a good boy. Your father said he's doing some renovation work."

"And are you okay about that?"

"*Koukla*, it's not the renovations I care about, it's the fact that your father won't agree to having a proper life with me. He's so tied up with vengeance for the Pattersons and a need to prove himself that he has lost sight of our happiness. He can do whatever he likes with the Palace now. I have no interest in it. Your father thinks I'm coming home with him this week, but I'm not going anywhere until he understands why I'm so upset."

"Morning."

Yasmin twisted to see Lane walk through the door. He wore dark pants and a checked shirt and tie, just as formal and together as ever. And just as always, her heart did a little leap when she saw him.

"Is that Lane? Oh, where is he? Can I speak to him?"

"Hey, Mrs. K." Lane stepped into her mother's line of vision, his face breaking into a broad smile.

"Oh, look how handsome you are in your business clothes, Lane! I was only saying to Maria this morning how lucky Yasmin is to have a man like Lane Griffiths looking out for her."

Yasmin shook her head and threw a look at Lane.

"Yasmin's the one who's on top of things here, Mrs. K," he said, throwing a smile back. "She seems to know exactly what she wants."

"I like her new hair, do you?"

"I'll call you again tonight, Mom," Yasmin said, desperate to get her mother off the call before she started asking Lane if he had a girlfriend.

"Okay, *koukla*. Big kisses."

Yasmin tapped her trackpad to close the window and turned back to look at Lane. It was only then that she noticed the person behind him.

"Yasmin, this is Paulo. He renovated my Mission restaurant a while back and still owes me a couple of favors, so he's going to work with us on the refurbishment."

Paulo. Tall, dark, handsome. He was well-built and a little disheveled, his eyes hidden behind a pair of smart, dark glasses. He was definitely not a go-get-'em businessman like Lane; more hardworking tradesman with an air of his own sexiness.

"Hey, Yasmin." Paulo took her hand and held it a second or two longer than was natural. He pushed the glasses onto his forehead and looked her directly in the eyes. "I bet this place has seen its fair share of romance, and with someone as beautiful as you in charge, how could it not?"

That was a line. Yes, that was definitely a pickup line. Yasmin's gaze skidded to Lane as she felt the heat crawling up her neck.

"Well, it would see romance, wouldn't it, being a wedding venue?" Lane said with a snort. He pulled out a chair for Yasmin, then sat next to her and indicated one on the other side of him for Paulo.

"This is a great old building," Paulo said when they were all seated. "I performed here once at a wedding." He had the tiniest hint of an accent.

"You're a singer?" she asked. He was almost too beautiful, and although he kept eye contact with her the whole time, she found her gaze shifting back to Lane.

"No, a dancer. I teach salsa in my spare time, and the bride and groom had come for lessons." He winked. "The bridesmaids were all keen on a demonstration after the first dance."

Lane cleared his throat and was laying papers on the table in front of them.

"Oh, I love salsa! Do you teach in town? I've been thinking about dance lessons." Three birds with one stone? Her list raced through her head: *learn a new language; tall, dark, and handsome; learn to dance.*

Paulo reached into his pocket and took out a card. "Please give me a call and we can arrange something." An eyebrow lifted. "It would be my pleasure."

She took the card and put it in her pocket.

"We're going to be far too busy in the next few weeks for there to be any dancing ... or any sort of fooling around." Lane didn't look at either of them, just pulled his chair in and spread the papers wider, a small frown on his forehead. "I'd appreciate it if I could have your attention. I've been thinking that one of the first things we should do is change the floor covering. I've used good marble ..."

Hmmmm. That comment about not fooling around was a direct result of her father asking Lane to look out for her, she was sure of it.

"Marble sounds good," she said, leaning a little closer to the papers on the table, trying to hide her irritation. "But wouldn't that be really expensive?"

"I have some left over from one of my jobs, and because Paulo owes me labor, we could do it reasonably cheaply."

"It sounds great. Very Mediterranean and a little opulent as well." At least he wasn't marching Paulo out of the place.

"It would certainly step up the feel of the Palace, look a little more like some of the wedding venues in those brochures."

"It would be great for dancing," Paulo said, and when she looked up he gave her a secret wink. "All that sliding around." He really was flirting with her, and part of her hoped that Lane had seen it.

"I was more concerned about it being easy to clean and functional than its suitability as a dance floor." Lane pulled out a brochure full of wall coverings. "We may change the acoustic tiles, as it'll be noisier with chairs being pushed in and out. These tiles would work."

"I was thinking about that." Yasmin leaned closer to the brochure and smelled freshly laundered shirt and male body beneath. Remembering his date tonight caused a sudden pang in her chest. He'd rejected her outright last night, there was no getting away from that, and she was going to have to imagine him with another woman, even if he did make it seem like they'd just be talking business.

"Or," Paulo chipped in, "we could find artworks to hang, something with a modern Greek theme."

"I have a few ideas," she said.

"Go ahead," Lane said.

"What if we changed the current tables and chairs to long tables and bench seats? It would make it more communal, more fun and funky, and could work equally as well on restaurant nights as wedding days," she said.

"No," Lane said. "Fun and funky isn't your parents' style, and I, for one, wouldn't want to be sitting next to a whole lot of people I didn't know when I went out for dinner. If we have the marble floor we can go for glass-topped round tables. We could have them plain for the restaurant and use white cloths for weddings."

Don't I get a say in this? She cleared her throat. "I, for one," she said, mimicking his disapproving tone, "don't like looking down at my thighs while I'm eating. Or anyone else's for that matter."

Paulo chuckled. "What about color schemes? These blacks and golds need to go. What do you think, Yasmin?"

"I'd like something fresh, something that looks like the ocean. Not turquoise, but maybe more a teal."

"Great choice," Paulo said.

There was a pause for a moment, and then Lane turned to look at her. "We don't want to overdo color. We could change up the texture of everything with brushed aluminum serving areas and detail on the walls. That will help with the acoustics, too."

She bit her lip. She'd wait until Paulo left before she pointed out to him that she'd like to have some say in the direction they were going, but for now she just wanted one thing they could agree on. "The grapevines will have to go. I kinda like them, though. They make it feel as though we're sitting outside under the stars. Hey, how cool would it be to have tiny lights shining through black cloth in the ceiling, so it did look like stars? Then the grapevines wouldn't look so out of place."

Lane was flipping through documents on the table. "Not cool at all, and definitely no grapevines."

He was the expert, but his conservative view of everything was driving her insane. "We do need to keep some of the Greek things." She looked around her. "Those statues take up a lot of space. Hey, I know ..."

She stopped as Lane gave her one of his looks that suggested whatever she was going to say next was going to be ridiculously loopy.

"What about we scrap the marble and go for a more relaxed feel? How about a polished concrete floor with mosaics laid into it? That would have the same sort of effect as marble, but it'd make everything feel more relaxed. And it would work perfectly with ... long wooden tables."

"That would look great," Paulo said. "You've got a talent for color and style, Yasmin." His voice became smoother. "You must be an artist."

"She's an expert in fungus." Lane had spoken without looking up.

"Oh ... like athlete's foot and things like that?" Paulo suddenly looked less interested in her.

"Dancers often get athlete's foot, don't you?" Lane asked. "You know the cracking and the stinging little cuts between your toes?"

"No, I don't ..."

"Seems like you're the only one who's experienced foot fungus, Lane." She raised her eyebrows at him and witnessed his fleeting grin before he looked serious again. "I study mushrooms, Paulo."

She'd never seen anyone look more relieved.

"So, Lane, what about the polished concrete floor?" she asked. "Is that going to clash with your vision?"

"I don't mind that idea," he said, "but it'd have too much of an impact on the rest of the weddings this summer. We can't afford to shut down the restaurant and have the dust and mess from grinding floors. We can't change the dates for weddings, so we need a quick and easy solution that won't cost much. What about plain wooden floors? They could be put down in a couple of days, and then we could use some carefully positioned rugs for extra texture."

They all nodded in agreement, and for the first time, Yasmin felt as though he wasn't cutting her down straightaway.

"Okay," Lane said to Paulo. "If you can liaise with Grace

about the best day to do it, we'll get this carpet taken up and the floor laid in as quick a time frame as possible. I'll also get Grace to explain the changes to the people who've booked weddings in the next couple of weeks to make sure they're happy, considering it'll be quite different from what they originally signed up for."

"Oh, and one other thing," Yasmin said. "I really hate those curtains. Is there a cheap but interesting option we can use for those?"

"I can source shutters that will give it a good Mediterranean feel, and we can add ceiling fans as well. You and I could go shopping together," Paulo said. "I know a great place."

"That would—"

"Yasmin will be too busy coordinating things here to go *shopping*," Lane said over the top of her. "And curtains will be better than shutters. You know the sort of thing I like, Paulo. Just send some photos from the suppliers. I'll call you about the floor tomorrow."

Yasmin slowly turned back to Lane and shook her head. Despite the fact that she wasn't really attracted to Paulo with all his winking and suggestion, it was clear that Lane didn't understand that, and that he'd do whatever he could to keep them apart. He really was prepared to act like a big brother while her father wasn't here. He was actually sitting there telling her who she would and wouldn't associate with. She couldn't wait until they were alone so she could explain to him exactly how she felt about *that*.

5

 hen they'd finished their meeting and Paulo had left, Lane stood, struggling not to show how difficult it had been watching Paulo flirt with Yasmin. They needed to discuss new menu options with Leo in the kitchen, but Yasmin didn't rise from her seat. He glanced at her and found her glaring at him, her face thunderous and eyes sparking.

"What was all that about?" she asked, folding her arms.

He rested a hand on the back of his chair. "The comment that you'd be too busy? The truth." No point mentioning the fire of jealousy that had licked through his veins every time Paulo had smiled at her.

Her stare shot angry little darts into him. "You didn't need to take that tone, as if Paulo had intentions other than treating me like the competent project manager that I'll be. Do you think I see this as some sort of game?" Her chin jutted forward a little and her rosy lips crinkled as she pressed them together. For the briefest second he wondered how soft those lips would be against his own when he kissed her, how her body would feel pressed along the length of his while they made love.

He lifted his briefcase and shook off the image. "Look, I'm not an expert in male-female communication, but I'd suggest that with all the winking and smirking that was going on, Paulo wanted to stroke a little more than furnishing fabrics with you." And the thought *still* made him bristle.

An indignant sound huffed from her mouth and for an awful moment he wondered if she'd seen through him.

He speared a hand through his hair and tried again. "I don't think you're treating this as a game, but we only have a short window to get things done and we don't have time to waste. Now, are we going to talk to Leo in the kitchen?"

She didn't move, just lifted her hand to the butterfly at her throat and stroked it. Why in all hell that singular movement kept getting him all steamed up, he didn't know.

"Not until we have this sorted properly," she said. "Not until we've established ground rules about how we're going to work together."

Ground rules? What is it with Yasmin and lists? He opened his mouth to get the conversation back on track, but she stopped him by holding up a hand.

"Up until now I think I've been pretty open to your rigid approach to all this." She stood and pushed her chair in.

Her bright orange top with sleeves like wings made her look as though she were a bird from the tropics about to take flight. It seemed a ridiculous thing to be wearing, but at the same time it suited her perfectly.

"Lane, I need your help to get the restaurant where we want it, but you can't dictate whom I see and when. If you're not interested in me I can accept that, but I won't have you acting as some sort of corporate babysitter. Are we clear?"

His heart clenched tight in his chest. This was all about his rejection of her last night—she'd believed he couldn't be interested in her, which was good, but seeing her so passionate and ready to stand up for herself made him even more sorry he'd had to turn her down.

Even if he couldn't be with her, Paulo wouldn't be the one to take his place. That man would never be right for someone as sweet as Yasmin. She deserved someone who saw all the honest possibilities in the world, a man who'd put her every whim first and understand her need for fun and laughter.

"So," he said pointedly, "you liked the way he was winking and smirking?"

She pulled her lip between her teeth then released it. "Not particularly, but that's not the point."

"It was sleazy, and if Paulo pulls anything like that again I'll be telling him so and he'll be off the project." He started to walk toward the kitchen, and thankfully, this time she followed.

She'd always been so quiet before, so studious and polite. This new assertiveness, as well as the self-confidence when she'd propositioned him last night, was becoming a turn-on, and he needed to get away from all this temptation, get the work at the Palace finished, and get back to his real life and the things that really made him happy.

"What you do with your time," he said over his shoulder, "won't be an issue, because you won't have any to spare. Neither of us will have time to socialize, or do anything outside the work we're doing on the renovation."

He pushed the swing door and held it open for her, but she stepped toward him, then stopped and put her hands on her hips, her chest thrust slightly forward. He became aware of a soft, floral scent surrounding her, and when she ran her tongue across her top lip he had to concentrate on what she was saying. "And will I get a say in any of the renovation?"

"Of course you will." And of course she could go where and with whomever she wanted. But now, something made him want to keep her here with him for the next couple of weeks. And it was precisely that lack of focus that he wouldn't succumb to. He couldn't let anything distract him. Especially not Yasmin.

Suddenly, her phone made its echoing doorbell sound. "And do you think you could change that damn ringtone while we're working together? I keep thinking there's a door-to-door salesman in your bag."

She was holding the phone in her hand and, for once, she didn't switch the sound off. "For your information, it isn't a ringtone, it's a mindfulness bell. A reminder to live in the moment, not to have regrets or to worry about the future. A reminder to appreciate what's happening in the here and now."

The way her cheeks flushed and her eyes shone caused him to hesitate on his response. A mindfulness bell to remind her to live in the moment? What a way to live a life.

What he wanted in this moment was to kiss her, lose himself in her, tangle his fingers in that ridiculous hair, and forget all about time.

But that would be wrong. People had to be sensible, have maturity in making decisions and look to the long term, to their goals, not merely live for the here and now.

"And another thing." She pushed a strand of hair back over her shoulder. "I don't want you to write off the idea of the long tables just yet," she said, gesturing back toward the restaurant. "I'd like to have the chance to show you how it could look."

He grinned; he couldn't help it. She wasn't backing

down, and good for her. "Okay, going out with who you want I'll agree to," he said, hoping like all hell it never happened, "as long as it doesn't interfere with what we're doing here. The long tables? Never."

She made a little noise in the back of her throat that wasn't wildly different from the sound of pleasure he'd heard when she'd eaten that scone at the tearoom. Irritatingly, he was dying to hear it again.

"Hello, kids!" Leo was walking toward them and waving his hands in the air, Boris trotting close behind him. He was like a smiling bear with a thick mop of hair standing up on his head. "Lane! *File mou!*" The slap to Lane's back almost sent him flying into a tray of tomatoes.

Lane held out his hand, glad of the temporary distraction from Yasmin. "Thanks for giving us your time again, Leo."

"No problem. I'm madly excited to change the menus. Pia liked to set them, and it's not easy to argue with her. To be honest, they haven't changed much at all since I've been here." He gave a wide-eyed look. "My sister scares me more than my own wife. I've come up with a few things for you to try from the list of ideas you sent. Come through, come through! Boris cat, you can stay here and I will give you the trimmings from the salmon later."

Lane looked back at Yasmin and her face had softened.

"We ate beautiful food last night, didn't we, Lane?" she said as they walked into the kitchen together. "There was a great stuffed vegetable dish, Leo, sort of like *yemista* but with orzo and gorgeous sharp cheese. The little meatballs were really tasty in an *avgolemono* sauce, and the marinated octopus was amazing."

Leo began removing his full-length apron. "Good, good, but I have to go out front. *Wedding World* want to take photos for the award I won at the artisan baker awards Saturday night. My special village bread was rated best in class! Can you imagine it! My old yiayia's recipe winning an award. Young Grace thinks my publicity will be good for the Palace." He waved an arm to indicate the array of dishes on the counter. "I've arranged a few things that I thought you might like to try." He hung the apron on a hook by the sink. "I'll be back in about half an hour and we can discuss which you think might work. From left to right we have a feta dip with dill, limes, and flatbread. Next to that is duck cakes with a yogurt dip, and in honor of our *koukla* Yasmin, there are *haloumi* and mushroom kebabs! Then a choice of main dishes: ground beef, mint, and pine nut pie; slow-roasted lemon and saffron chicken thighs; and pork with orzo, roast figs, and Asian greens. Finally, your dessert choices, caramelized sugar pudding with persimmon and mint, and chocolate and fig baklava."

When Leo had left, Lane pulled up a stool for Yasmin and one for himself. "Feel like eating at the same table as me, or would you rather tip that sauce over my head?"

She narrowed her eyes at him, but her mouth tilted in a grin. "Don't tempt me. How much nicer it would be if we were eating at a long table, though ..."

He chuckled. "Long tables can be the source of all sorts of diseases. Athlete's foot for starters."

She swiped at the air above his head and pulled the plates closer. "Yes, thanks for the way you explained my work to Paulo. If he had been interested in me that was sure to turn him right off."

"Precisely," he said, slanting her an unapologetic grin.

"Are you sure you're happy to eat this today?" Her tone was teasing as she waved a hand across the plates in front of them. "I thought you might have another sandwich stowed in that briefcase."

He laughed. *She gave as good as she got.* "I like to be prepared, though today I knew I'd be eating here, so no, Monday's chicken salad on oat bran was canceled."

She looked at him for a second, shook her head, then turned back toward the table. "My God, how good does this food look? I'm getting so excited about all this. Mom feels pretty passionate about the food we serve, but everyone has always been scared to question her choices. She loves you too much to ignore you telling her we need to change the menu."

Lane's gaze flicked to hers and he swallowed. Did she know what a comment like that meant to him? Or that it reminded him he had to keep her at a distance?

Lane took a piece of warm flatbread and spread a little of the dip on it before passing it to her. "We need to confirm a relaunch date. It's important that we don't take too much time on the renovation. We don't want your parents coming back to a mess, and we want to be able to build anticipation, so we'll need to let all the media know when it's going to be. Sooner rather than later."

Yasmin took a bite of the pita and dip, and for the next minute there was silence as her eyes closed and she started chewing. His skin heated as he watched, and in that moment he wanted nothing more than to be the one who put that expression on her face.

When she'd finished the bread, Yasmin took a bite of the ground beef pie, the fine, buttery phyllo pastry falling like snowflakes onto her chin and top. There was a creamy but tangy filling of ricotta cheese, pine nuts, and herbed ground beef and it all worked beautifully. Leo had outdone himself. She looked at Lane, so calm and together, and her heart squeezed as she remembered his rejection of her last night. What a waste.

"So, what sort of thing did you have in mind to celebrate the relaunch? I'm not sure that Mom and Dad will be back as soon as Dad had hoped."

He rubbed his fingers across his mouth and paused before he spoke. "Hopefully, they'll be here well before. Obviously it'll be held in the restaurant. We'll need to do a Sunday or Monday night when weddings aren't booked and the restaurant is closed. We'll have all the furnishings complete, the new tables and chairs, and we'll serve a selection of the new menu. I need to talk to Grace, but we could also have new flower designers represented, a dramatic-looking cake or two, something that's going to really make the media sit up and take notice of the huge changes here."

"And a time frame?"

"Two weeks."

Yasmin nearly blew a mouthful of phyllo over him. "But you said you had a month!"

"I did, but if we leave it too much later we'll be getting toward the end of summer. We want to be able to maximize covers in the restaurant every night, and have the place looking great for all the potential new clientele who'll be scoping out places for their summer weddings next year and beyond."

"How are we going to get things done in that time with the restaurant still open until eleven p.m. most nights?"

He reached over and speared a green vegetable. "We'll book the tradespeople to work early morning until mid afternoon, then they'll need to tidy everything away. And you and I will work nights after the dinner crowd have left to do the more straightforward jobs like painting and staging."

She stuck her lip out and gave him a mock pout. "I'll never survive those hours." Her doctor's insistence that she get plenty of rest echoed in her head.

"It's only fourteen nights, and you'll be able to sleep in the early part of the day as Grace will have everything under control. We'll have the whole of next Monday as well."

Yasmin picked up a fork and reached for a piece of chicken. Having Lane keep an eye on her shouldn't be something to encourage now that he'd made his feelings for her clear. But she smiled secretly to herself. Who was she to stop him from doing his duty? That the eye-keeping would be happening during late evenings when no one else was around wasn't something she was going to argue with, either. She could quite happily look at him 24-7.

And since he was in a fairly open mood, she wanted to understand him a little more. "Tell me, honestly, why are you so committed to doing all this? From what Grace was telling me, you're pretty successful."

He was looking directly in her eyes and her heart did its familiar pitter-pat. "Because your Dad asked me to. Here, do you want to try the yogurt sauce with that?"

She nodded and he spooned some of the creamy mixture onto her plate.

"I know, but taking time out from your own life—the days and now the nights—is pretty dedicated."

He shrugged. "It's just what friends do. I owe your family, Yasmin. When I was a kid, Nick and your family were the only people I could count on in my life." Even though he tried to cover it, there was hurt in his voice. "Part of me used to feel as though everything in the world revolved around the Palace and the Katsalos family. Like your family was the sun and everything else was only worthy of orbiting it."

An overwhelming urge to reach out and touch him overtook her, but she fought it and put her palm flat on the table. He wouldn't want her sympathy. "I'd have thought my family was a lot less like the sun, and more like a pile of space junk hurtling haphazardly through its own universe into a yawning black hole."

He gave her the briefest of smiles, but it didn't reach his eyes. "It was a good, solid piece of space junk."

"Were you here for all the raised voices and the threats to disown one another?" she asked, throwing her hands around the way her family did when conversations got heated.

He shrugged, but not with his usual casual confidence; there was something deeper going on behind his eyes. "I came to understand that the raised voices were about passion, and the threats to disown one another were just another way to say you couldn't live without one another. I'd have given anything to have that sort of thing in my own family."

The tight tone to his voice betrayed an old pain, and more than anything, she wanted to take it away for him. Giving in to the need for connection that her body demanded, she reached out a hand and touched the crisp cotton of his shirtsleeve. "I'm sorry. I didn't mean to make light of what you went through with your own family. I know I take for granted what I had. I think that's part of the reason Mom went back to Greece. We'd all been taking one another for granted for far too long."

He looked down at her hand and then up into her eyes, and her pulse began to quicken. Now it made sense. Why he'd rejected her last night. He didn't want to mess up his friendship with Nick, didn't want to run the risk of losing touch with her family if something went wrong between the two of them. Suddenly she felt like the most selfish person in the world for even suggesting a fling with him. He felt like there was too much to lose. She gently removed her hand and laid it in her lap.

"That's the whole crazy thing." He rubbed a hand down his face and let out a breath. "I didn't go through anything particularly bad with my family. I just didn't have much of one. Neither of my parents was in a relationship again after they split when I was young, so I remained the focus for both of them, and a lot of that focus was about who was doing the best parenting, whose place did I want to spend the most time at? My whole childhood was about scoring points and one-upmanship. It was a relief to come to the Palace where people talked about other things, played practical jokes, and stuck up for one another." He smiled at her again, and this time it was genuine. "That's the sort of family I want to have one day."

She didn't want to dig too deep and ask him to lay more of his pain bare, but she was fascinated about one thing. "Do you think it's affected the way you'll want to be as a parent?"

He carefully laid his fork on one of the empty plates. "Absolutely. No child of mine will be moved around all the time. I want a stable place for them to live, predictable and constant parents. I want to work hard to give them a comfortable life, and live near family so we can create bonds and lasting memories, not to feel isolated and alone." He rubbed two fingers over the frown lines that had appeared on his forehead. "I intend to give my kids everything I didn't have."

Yasmin thought about her own future. Did she even want children? If she eventually did decide to have them, she'd want them to travel the world with her. Even when she was studying full time, she'd always imagined breaking free one day, living life on her own terms, and she wanted that for any family she might have. They really were completely different—well, at least to the way she was now.

She took another piece of bread, marveling at the fact that something they'd shared—the experience of life with the Katsalos family—had impacted them so differently. She couldn't help but be disappointed they were people who dreamed of such different futures.

"I can't believe he turned you down!" Genie said as the hair stylist twisted her hair up into an elaborate do the following day. "Is he nuts? Look at you with your gorgeous, fresh style and your new confidence. What other man would pass up the opportunity of a relationship with this?" She waved her finger in the air in front of Yasmin.

"I think the fact that it's me is scaring him off," Yasmin said as she played with one of the stylist's hair combs. "That if things ended badly between us it could damage his friendship with Nick, and my whole family for that matter. If I was anyone but a Katsalos, he might be tempted."

"But you weren't exactly asking him to walk down the aisle with you, you ... Ow!"

"Sorry," the hairdresser said, flinching. "Those combs have quite sharp ends."

"No kidding ..." Genie gave her a dark look and then turned her attention back to Yasmin. "I mean, you weren't asking for anything long term. And why would your family have to know? Maybe you just need to say to him that it would be short and sweet and no one else would find out. Alternatively," she said with a cheeky grin, "you could ask him to take you to the nude rodeo and see how things develop from there. Have you told him he has a duty to help you fulfill one particular item on your list?"

"Yes, I have." Yasmin bit down on her lip as she remembered their conversation. "I felt a bit silly at first, but he seemed interested that I'd have that as a priority."

"Of course he did. It's super sexy to have someone tell you that you fit all their criteria for a fling. Imagine if a guy said that to you." She put on a low and sultry voice. "My whole life I've wanted to spend one night with a woman with purple streaks in her hair and a kick-ass attitude. Take me now or my life will be incomplete."

Yasmin chuckled. "I just don't think I'd ever fit on any list of Lane's. Unless it was for a career-focused woman with good table manners, or as a member of his favorite family. He's so serious and stable, and he has such firm views on everything. He's all or nothing. You've got to admit that I'm hardly like that anymore."

She thought about the connection she could feel growing between her and Lane though, the teasing, the laughing, the working on something so important together. Maybe there *was* too much to lose. "I don't know, maybe it was a silly thing to do—put seducing a tall, dark man on my list."

"It wasn't silly at all. You've always had the hots for him, and if I'm not mistaken, that feeling has only increased since you met up again. I think you should give it another shot. Let him know that you're only after a little fun and I bet he'll change his mind. No man I've ever met would have been able to resist a line like that."

"Close your eyes." The hair stylist held up a can of hair spray and sprayed a cloud around Genie's head. "Hang on and I'll get a mirror to show you the back."

When she'd gone, Genie leaned closer. "I look ridiculous, don't I? My hair looks like one of those boy wigs from the seventeenth century. The ones that had all the maggots wriggling underneath because people would never wash them." She pulled a disgusted face and then scratched her head vigorously. "This hairdresser is a friend of Carmel's mother, so I can't say anything, but sheesh, it looks bad."

Yasmin grinned at her friend. "It's not your usual wild style, but I'm sure it'll look beautiful with your bridesmaid's dress."

Genie suddenly grabbed Yasmin's arm. "Don't tell me Lane's not coming to the wedding now that he's said no. We have to have you with a date, or my cousin Bernie will be after you like he was at my twentieth birthday party."

"No, he's still coming." She lowered her voice. "We're going to use it as a bit of an undercover sting to find out what the Pattersons are doing so right with their place. We might get a few ideas for decorating the restaurant and improving our service from it."

"Oh, great idea. I heard that their daughter Erin, you know that really classy girl from school, has taken over running the place."

The hairstylist came back and held up the mirror, and Genie touched the back of her head. "Yeah, it'll do. After I get my hands on the groomsman it'll be all messed up anyway."

The hairdresser gave a disapproving look, then removed the towel and cape around Genie's shoulders, and as she stood, she shook all over like a horse having its saddle removed. "My only piece of advice about next weekend is to wear the sexiest dress you have. What man doesn't get swept away by the romance and open bar of a wedding that's not his own?"

Yasmin did a mental inventory of her closet. "I don't know if I've got anything suitable. Want to come shopping?"

"Of course. How about after this?"

"Sorry, I can't. Lane's picking me up from here in a minute. We're going to look at fabric for the new restaurant drapes and chair coverings."

Genie lifted an eyebrow.

"What?"

"I didn't have Lane pegged as an expert in soft furnishings, not with his suits and that briefcase you say he keeps carrying around."

Yasmin laughed. "He's not. I think the only reason he's taking me is to stop me from going with Paulo."

"Paulo? Who? What the—!?"

The door to the salon opened and Lane stepped in. "Hi." He pulled sunglasses from his face and as usual, Yasmin's heart beat *tippity-tap* against her rib cage. She hadn't seen him since their discussion about why he was doing all this for her father, and somehow, knowing how strongly loyal he was to her brother and her family made her want him all the more.

"Genie, you remember Lane," Yasmin said.

"Great to see you again, Lane." Genie beamed. "I don't normally look like a trussed-up turkey, but lucky you, you get to see me like this again at the wedding!"

Lane grinned. "Great hair, and I'm looking forward to your brother's wedding."

She gave an exaggerated whisper. "It's so cool, you guys going on an undercover recon mission. Just let me know if you need me to distract anyone. Unless of course I'm too busy with my own grab-the-groomsman mission."

"I appreciate the offer," Lane said, chuckling, then turned to Yasmin. "Are you ready? The car's outside."

Yasmin nodded, then gave Genie a hug, and her best friend whispered in her ear, "Short, sweet, and no strings, remember. Go on, give it another try."

Fifteen minutes later they were standing in the Bella Casa fabric warehouse. Rows and rows of colorful bolts of fabric stretched out in the building as big as two football fields and suddenly Yasmin felt out of her depth. Maybe she should've talked to her mom about this? Maybe she should've taken advice from a real interior designer rather than trusting her own taste and the practical know-how of a man like Lane.

"You really didn't need to come with me, you know," she said. "I can't imagine you've had much to do with fabric before." She stroked the enormous roll next to her. It was a light, gauzy material that felt rough under her fingers.

He nodded. "True, but I know what will work well in the restaurant in terms of creating the right atmosphere."

"How was your date last night?" Yasmin said, pretending to be fascinated by a packet of curtain rings, while she held her breath for his reply.

"I thought I told you it wasn't a date. Lisa and I were meeting about the charity food organization we run."

Genie's speech about giving it another try with Lane echoed in Yasmin's ears. If last night hadn't been a date, and if she could suggest something short, sweet, and discreet, maybe his response this time would be different.

"May I help you?" A middle-aged woman in a well-cut

suit and fine gold glasses appeared from behind one of the rolls. *Marilyn. How can I be of service?* was stamped on a large name tag on her chest.

"We're looking for curtain fabric for a wedding hall," Lane explained. "Neutral, serviceable, and a color that will go with white walls. Probably a navy blue or dark brown."

"Navy? Brown?" Yasmin said, turning to face him. "It's a wedding hall, not a funeral hall. We'll be wanting to see soft colors," she said to Marilyn. "A girl wants to feel she's in a fairy tale when she's at her wedding, and that's all about having everything look shimmery and ethereal."

The woman looked from Yasmin back to Lane. "Which one of you is in charge of the money?"

"I am," they both said, turning to glare at each other.

"Who's done this before, then?" The woman looked as though she was fed up with arguing couples.

Yasmin looked at Lane, but he was already focused on Marilyn. "I have. Many times."

"In that case we'll go to the darker colors." She led the way and Lane followed her.

"We can't have something boring, Lane. It should look regal," Yasmin said as they made their way through the linen section, and then past stripes.

"You'll have to trust me on this," he said and carried on following Marilyn.

"We'll have the white walls and the lightness of the polished floors. That'll all get swamped by dark-colored linen on the windows and chairs."

They stopped in front of a tower of fabric bolts in beiges, browns, and taupes.

Yasmin picked up the corner of a piece of rich, heavy fabric and rubbed it between her fingers. "But it's so neutral, so predictable. What about something to match the bride and the whiteness of the walls. What about a textured white? That would be amazing with rugs and new artwork. What do you think?"

The woman had her lips pressed together as if she'd dealt with silly women with nose studs every day but would always get the better of them.

"How about this?" Yasmin ran over to a cylinder of steely blue silk, the color of the sea on an autumn day. She draped the end length across herself and then pulled a piece of gauzy tulle from the roll above over her head. "Doesn't this make everything look ethereal and dreamy? Can't you imagine how beautiful that would be with all the other changes we're making?"

"Do the weddings you go to invite children?" Lane asked. He and the woman were staring at her as if she'd completely lost her mind.

Yasmin eyed him suspiciously. "Of course."

"And have you seen the way kids seem to get their hands into every potted plant, every buffet table? Can you imagine what your floaty dream fabric would look like with a few dozen ketchup mouths and dirty noses wiped on it?"

She winced. He had a point, but just because something needed to be serviceable, it didn't need to be ugly. "What about this one then?" She dropped the blue piece she'd been holding and picked up a piece of richly textured and heavy fabric in a dove gray.

The saleswoman looked at Lane and shrugged. "I think you could have a battle on your hands, hon. I'll leave you to discuss this for a few moments." She turned and hurried off.

6

$\mathcal{Y}$ asmin stood with a soft piece of white fabric over her hair and a silver-gray piece stretched across her middle looking like an excited bride, a woman who knew exactly what she wanted, and it was driving Lane wild. She had a determined look on her face, eyes like saucers, and a grin at her perfect mouth.

"It looks good on you, if that helps." Lane stepped forward and touched the material. "And I know you want everything to be completely different, but it's just not going to work. There's no point in being different just for the sake of it."

"What do you mean by that?" Her eyes had narrowed, but he couldn't help the smile that pulled at the corner of his mouth at the sight of her. Her enthusiasm was almost infectious. If he didn't know how important sensible and conservative decisions were in business, he'd say yes just to see the excitement that was sure to beam across her face.

He took the gray fabric from her middle and put it on a display table. "I know you're on this mission to break rules and push boundaries, but there are other places you can do it besides your parents' business."

"Maybe you're right." Her shoulders sagged. "See, even though you drive me crazy with your belief that there's only one way to do everything, I'd never have thought of noses being wiped on a curtain."

"I might know about the hospitality industry, but I'm sure there are just as many rules of engagement when you're studying mushrooms."

"I guess," she said. "But that won't help our project."

"You know, I had a question about that. About that little toadstool." Actually, he'd been thinking too much about her sitting in the woods surrounded by cute little toadstools, like something out of a fairy tale. "Why is it called the amethyst deceptor?"

"It's the amethyst *deceiver*, and it's called that because at first it starts out with a beautiful purple color that makes it really easy to distinguish, but then over time it fades to look like any other fungus, so you have to know what you're looking for."

"It sounds complex." And unexpectedly intriguing. Just as she was.

She sighed. "Not as complex as choosing fabric."

He laughed and lifted the material that was now sitting like a veil across her hair. "I hate to tell you what my dry-cleaning bills have been for curtains in my restaurants, and that doesn't factor in the ones that get pulled down when people get over-vigorous with their celebrating."

She looked up at him and her eyes danced. How could it be fair that someone who was so smart and beautiful and determined was so off-limits? Or that he'd never have the focus to invest in someone like her? He tucked the fabric back into the roll and she smoothed down her dress.

"What about gold?" he said, wanting to make up for her disappointment. "That would hide some finger marks but might give you the look you want."

"Maybe." She flicked her hair over her shoulder and peered around the end of the bolt tower. "Do you think we should call Marilyn back? She kinda makes me feel like a bull in a china shop."

He joined her at the end of the row and they carefully looked around again together. "No, let's do it ourselves."

For the next fifteen minutes, they walked through the maze of towering fabric bolts, stopping every time Yasmin saw something that took her fancy—a canary yellow and magenta stripe, a dizzying pattern of French botanicals with a blue background. At each one she'd stop and stroke it, turning puppy-dog eyes to Lane. Finally they came to an area surrounded by every shade of gold imaginable.

"Ohhhhhh." That noise of pleasure at the back of her throat again. "Lane, this is *beautiful*," she said, and she picked up the corner of fabric. "Look how rich it is. It's textured and a little bit shimmery." She played with the weight of it in her hand. "And I think it would fall beautiful-ly." She lifted it to her face and breathed. "And it smells all fresh and linen-y."

"Let's hope that's the closest it gets to anyone's nose." He stepped closer and rubbed a piece between his fingers. "Feels good. Let's take a look at the price tag."

Beside him, she stretched up on tiptoe as he brought the tag closer.

"Thirty dollars per yard. Not too bad. I think we might've found what we're looking for."

"Oh my God, you're a genius!" She reached an arm around his shoulders and when he turned back to look at her, they both froze.

He gazed down into her warm brown eyes and was sucker punched by the excitement and joy he found there. This was about so much more than fabric and decorating to her. This was about self-expression and wearing her heart on her sleeve, exactly the things that made him feel as though he was in unchartered territory. He was so logical and sensible and Yasmin was ... not. But he didn't care. In this instant he needed to get as close to her as he could; he wanted some part of her zest for life and her crazy, naive excitement to brush off on him.

From somewhere in her handbag came the sound of her mindfulness bell. It was a call to the moment, a signal to forget about the past, to not worry about the future. Maybe it was even a call for him to let go of everything and lose himself in her.

Before he could decide, she pulled his head down to hers and kissed him. Her lips were cool and moist, her breathing rapid, and when she made that noise at the back of her throat again, he knew he couldn't pull away. He backed her into the stack of fabric rolls opposite, all the while kissing her mouth.

He heard the rolls wobble, but he didn't care. A tide of sensations overpowered him. The clean, freshly laundered scent of the fabrics surrounding them, the sound of her body brushing up against the silk roll behind her, and the dazed look on her face when she finally pulled her lips from his was priceless.

"Lane," she whispered. "I don't want you to get in trouble." Her brown eyes were wide, her breathing rapid.

"I'm living in the moment," he said and brushed his hand down the soft skin of her cheek. He didn't want to talk or think, just wanted to taste those dusky lips, so he leaned in and kissed her again.

This time she hooked both hands around his neck and kissed him deeper, and he played along her lip with his tongue until it met hers in a delicate dance. When her fingers played up the back of his neck, a shudder ripped through his body. He looped his arm around her waist and dragged her into him so her breasts were pressed to his chest, and as heat radiated between them, his pulse beat hard at his neck.

For a second, Yasmin lost her balance and a roll behind her back dislodged the next one down. Her lips formed a grin against his mouth as she whispered. "Forget it. Don't stop. Please don't stop."

Somehow, she'd freed his shirt from his jeans and when her fingers touched his skin he sucked in a sharp breath. Never had he wanted anyone so much or so deeply. But he wanted more, needed more—

"I do hope you realize that any damage to the fabrics will be charged in full."

They sprang apart, and the shop assistant was looking at them disapprovingly over the top of her glasses. "Body oils can leave permanent stains on such fine material."

Yasmin swung her gaze to him and looked as though she was about to burst into laughter. He was still trying to get the blood back to his brain, so humor and thought were impossible.

"I take it you've finally agreed on a shade," Marilyn said, her lips pursed.

Lane cleared his throat and straightened his collar. He felt like a schoolboy who'd been caught kissing a girl behind the bleachers. The scent of Yasmin was still light across his skin, and each time he breathed, the essence of her was lost a little more.

"Oh, yes, we like the feel of this one, don't we, Lane?"

Yasmin said as a great, beaming smile glowed across her face.

Lane averted his eyes from Marilyn and suppressed a smile before standing straighter and pulling himself together. He managed to ask for a sample of the gold fabric, and after they'd talked quantities and price, she promised to come to the Palace and measure up, then thanked them for their business.

When they were finally finished, Lane followed Yasmin out to the car.

"I'm sorry about that," she said when they reached his convertible. "I got a bit carried away with all the excitement, and you looked so gorgeous among all that silk and satin." She bit her lip. "I hope it doesn't put you in an awkward position."

He flicked his sunglasses down onto his face, partly to avoid the glare of the midday sun, and partly so Yasmin couldn't see the effect she was having on him. "No harm done."

"No one would have to know about us, you know," she said softly. "Not Nick, not your friends or my parents. I know why you don't want anything to happen between us, that you're worried about what my family's reaction would be, but why does anyone have to know?"

Need still thrummed in his blood, urging him to take what she was offering. He managed to hold firm, but he couldn't look at her. "They'd find out eventually."

"Not if we didn't want them to. We could take things at our own pace, and if we're both still into it after a while, we could think about it then. We could just focus on it being a fling for now."

He straightened his spine, steeling himself against her

invitation. What was the point of a fling? Flings, by definition, had an end date, and where would that leave them? Awkward when they were around each other again, regretful that they'd crossed an invisible line that they couldn't get back again. No matter how fresh that incredible kiss still was in his mind and on his mouth, or that the only thing he wanted to do right now was press her against a wall and feel her body beneath his, he couldn't see this as ending any other way than very badly.

"Yas, Paulo's crew has finished with the floor. Do you want to come see?" Lane was looking at her from around the office door, his hair a little mussed.

It was late Wednesday afternoon, the only day for the next week without a wedding, and with no restaurant bookings either, Paulo's workmen had been installing the new floor.

"Okay, I'll be there in a minute." Grace had asked her opinion on the new advertising, but it could wait. She dropped the papers and turned back, but he'd already gone. Her chest hollowed. He seemed to be doing that a lot— appearing and disappearing. Though it was less about him doing it in the flesh and more about him only letting her see parts of himself for a short time before pulling them back behind his walls again.

She sighed and rubbed her tired eyes. For the first time since she'd been back, she felt quite weak and exhausted. She'd slept late after they worked into the night. Since the kiss at the store yesterday, she'd been unsure of where things sat with Lane. He was friendly and pleasant when they worked together, but nothing more had been said about the kiss, and she couldn't help feeling that he'd be quite happy if it was never referred to again.

Maybe he wished it hadn't happened at all.

But that lingering kiss had played over and over in her head, setting her nerves alight each time. The memory of how his body fitted, warm and firm, against her own had become intoxicating, and she wanted it to happen again. Maybe the fact that she was holding back about her illness was acting as a barrier between them. Perhaps she should really open up and tell him everything that had happened to her. Maybe then everything would fall away between them and he'd pull her close and do all the things she was imagining.

She made her way over to the restaurant, passing Paulo and his workmen on their way out. "I hope you like it, Yasmin," Paulo said with a wink. "There's plenty of room for dancing. Give me a call when you want a lesson."

"I'm sure it looks great. Thanks so much for all your hard work." She shook his outstretched hand. "I'll give you a call sometime."

"I'm counting on an invitation to the relaunch," he said and gave her another smile. "I've got a date I'd like to bring, too, if that's okay."

"We'd love to see you both." Yasmin grinned back. Paulo had never really been attracted to her; he was just one of those guys who couldn't help flirting with any girl he met. She hoped his date could see through that.

"Mano, I'll wring that bird's neck!" Monty said as she passed his cage. She dug her hand in her pocket for the peanuts that she'd gotten used to carrying around. He flew with one in his beak to his perch and chewed it noisily. "Pardon me," he said when he'd finished. "Toast the bride, toast the bride!"

She opened the door to the restaurant to see Lane standing in the middle of the brand-new floor, his black pants rolled up and nothing but socks on his feet. Even though he'd been helping with the physical work all afternoon, apart from his slightly disheveled hair, he still looked as composed as ever. Her fingers itched to ruffle it—and him —to be the one who made him lose his composure, just like he had against those rolls of fabric. Perhaps even undo his buttons and run her hands across the warm expanse of his skin before tossing his shirt to the floor.

Paulo's men had laid the pre-polished floor through the night and had spent the morning putting a final coat of wax on it. It had hues of honey and gold that cast a warm glow onto the walls. It was the perfect choice.

In one corner, Boris was batting a rolled-up piece of paper, then chasing it.

"Wow," she said, and the word echoed around the room, causing her to laugh. "It's amazing." With all the tables they'd moved out after the dinner service last night, it was light and airy.

"What do you think?" Lane said, hands on hips.

"It's gorgeous." She bent down and slid her hand across the smooth wood. "And so slippery."

"You can't wear shoes on it yet, apparently. It's bare feet or socks."

"How will it stand up to high heels, then?"

"Fine," he said, nodding. "We used a very hard wood that won't mark at all. We just can't put anything heavy or sharp on it for twenty-four hours because of the wax."

Yasmin pulled off the electric-blue wedges that had been killing her all day and sighed as her hot feet met the cool of the wood floor.

93

"They've done a great job," Lane said, crouching down to inspect it.

"What do we have to do to take care of it?"

"Not much, just a coat of polish every now and again."

Yasmin slid her feet along one of the boards. "Have you tried a little slide?"

He frowned at her as if she was speaking another language. "Sorry?"

"Before I got here," she said patiently, "did you take a run up and skid across the floor?"

"No." He gave her that look he'd given her a lot in the beginning, as if she was a little bit deranged and he hadn't been able to work out why he'd been stuck with her.

His reaction just made her want to be fun and spontaneous all the more. She crossed her arms under her breasts. "Then I really think you should."

"What?" He shook his head as if to rid himself of the nonsense she was talking. "Now the floor's down we need to move quickly to cover it up so we can finish off the painting. It would have been preferable to get the floor down after we'd painted to minimize accidents, but this is a crazy schedule we're working to."

"Then it's vital that we test the skidability of the floor before we cover it all up with rugs and drop sheets. Go on, I dare you." He was already walking over to the first wall that needed painting, the enormous mural of Santorini.

"I'm not doing any sort of sliding." He'd pulled a tape measure out of his suit pocket.

"Then take your socks off."

He turned back and looked at her, incredulous. "Pardon?"

She walked closer and held out her hand. "To save me going all the way back to the apartment to find some socks,

94

just give me yours. This floor is begging to be slid on, and if you won't do it, I'll have to."

He rolled his eyes at her, but she held his gaze.

He looked down at his socks. "They probably stink after a day of work. And they'd be way too big. Your feet are all tiny and delicate. Let's just get on with covering it up so we can start painting."

She lifted a shoulder and grinned. "I grew up with two brothers, remember. My sense of smell was obliterated years ago. But one thing they did teach me was how to master a perfect floor slide. And thanks, that's the nicest thing anyone's ever said to me about my feet. Now give me your socks

∼

"You're completely mad. You know that, don't you?" He shook his head but bent down, put the tape measure on the floor, and started to remove one of his black socks.

Everything happened on a whim for her, and it made him crazy. And ever so slightly jealous. What must it feel like to just do whatever you wanted, whenever the mood hit you? What would that sense of freedom, that blowing in the face of convention, feel like? If the look on her face was anything to go by, it'd feel pretty damn good.

Yasmin removed the cropped jacket she was wearing over a sunny yellow dress and took the sock from him, smiling. "You know you want to do it. I can see the thrill in your eyes."

She sat down to put the first sock on while he removed the second one. Finally, he was standing barefoot and she held out her hand for him to help her up.

"I'll expect you to fix any holes you put in them," he said

gruffly as he pulled her up.

"Life's too short to darn socks," she said with a grin. She looked so perfect with her simple yellow dress, her purple and black hair caught in a turquoise head scarf. With his black socks pulled up on her smooth calves, she looked like something out of an alternate Disney fairy tale. All he could focus on was those lips he'd kissed yesterday and the feel of her arms looped around his neck. A second too late he realized he'd been holding her hand too long, and he hurriedly dropped it and put his own behind his back.

He'd justified the kiss at the fabric store as Yasmin being carried away with the excitement of the drapes. He felt he'd dealt with it successfully.

She gave him a wink and then started moving away, pushing her feet out like she was an Olympic ice skater. When she reached the far side of the room she turned and leaned against the wall. "Okay, here goes!" She started to run, gaining speed so that the head scarf flitted out behind her. When she reached the middle of the room, she threw her arms out, twisted her body to the left and went sliding all the way to the other wall.

"Woohoo!" she cried. "Can you imagine what it's going to be like when we use this as a dance floor? I want to see Paulo in here doing a few of his salsa moves. And all the little kids who come to weddings, they're going to *love* it."

The high, musical tone of her voice echoed around the walls and high ceilings until it almost felt as though her voice was playing in his head. He smiled. How could a twenty-four-year-old sound thrilled about simply sliding across a floor? He had no idea, but damn if it wasn't making his heart beat stronger.

She set off again, reached the middle, then let out a whoop as she made it to the other side. "Wanna go?" she panted as she struck a pose like a sprinter and then set off across the floor once again. "I'll give you your socks back if you promise you'll do it just once."

"Plenty more black socks where those came from. You're welcome to them." He knew he should've been measuring the wall for painting, knew that time was precious and that they didn't have time for screwing around, but he couldn't stop watching her. God, what was it that made her so captivating? That made him feel lighter when he was with her?

It was true that he was fascinated by the ballsy way she dressed as she liked, putting color matches together that should've been illegal. And it was also true that he enjoyed hearing her talk about her love for her family and her friends, her studies, and the things she was passionate about. But the thing that made her so captivating and so easy to be around was that everything was just fun for her.

Never in a million years would he've thought about sliding across this floor in nothing but his socks, but to a woman like Yasmin, it was the most natural thing in the world.

Finally, she stood against the far wall, her hand digging into her side as if she had a stitch, her breath coming in quick bursts. "I used to come in here as a little girl, the night before a wedding," she said, then paused to get more breath. "I wasn't allowed to. Mom would have killed me if she'd known, but it was just so magical. I'd sneak in and turn the lights on and the glasses would sparkle and the silverware shine. Flowers would've been delivered and arranged and it smelled like one long springtime."

"You don't feel too sad about painting over this, then?" He gestured at the mural they were about to begin work on. "This room is going to look a whole lot different with that gone."

She gave a small shrug and a sad expression spread across her face. He wanted to go over and lift her, sock-clad feet and all, off the ground in a big hug. In fact, she looked quite pale and drawn. Was he pushing her too hard? Was all of this starting to be too much for her?

Slowly she slid toward him. "I talked to Dad about it over the weekend and he thinks it's a good idea. He's so desperate to get Mom to come home with him, he'll do whatever he can. It's sad, really," she said, her voice becoming wistful. "This whole place represents so much to him. One of my uncles painted that, but he's long gone now."

She'd drawn closer. Her cheeks had a rosy blush and strands of hair were falling from beneath her head scarf. "You don't think it's too late, do you?" A tiny frown dug into her forehead as she held his gaze.

"Too late?"

"To save this place. To save my parents. You don't think we're wasting our time here, do you?"

He started to speak, saying something about hard work and good management, but she shook her head.

"Without the diplomatic businessman thing you do so well, Lane. What does your heart tell you about this place? What do you think deep down about what's going on here?" She put her hand across her own heart and he remembered the scent of her when they'd kissed. How her hair had smelled of flowers and sunshine.

He swallowed. What did he feel deep down? Deep down he knew he had inappropriate feelings for his best friend's little sister. Deep down he felt that if he screwed things up between them he could lose the whole of the Katsalos family. And deep down he wondered when the next time would be that he could pull her into his arms and taste her sweet lips on his. He'd begun to dream about slipping the straps of her dress down, of sliding the silky fabric of her skirt up her thighs until he could pull her hips closer.

"You don't need to sugarcoat it for me."

He put his hands on his hips and tried to keep his focus on the project. "I've got to admit, I'm a little worried that after all this hard work that you've done, after all the time and energy you've put into it, you might not get what you want and the Palace might have to be sold."

Suddenly, the light in her eyes dulled and she lifted her hand to gently touch the butterfly necklace at her throat. His arms ached to hold her while he told her everything would be all right, to comfort her. But he was simply her brother's friend. Her project partner. He could best help her by remaining focused on the project so they could ensure its success.

He cleared his throat and managed to find his business tone again. "But that's only going to happen if we spend our time sliding across floors and chatting up workers. If we put decent time and hard work into it, we might be able to pull it off. I have a plan to invite the press in a few days before the launch to get some early publicity, so we can't waste any more time."

She looked up at him through her lashes and he made the choice right there and then to step away and get on with the painting. It was the only sensible thing he could do. Though, for the first time in his life, he hated having to be the sensible one.

He curled his fingers into the palm of his hand and made himself a promise. He would find a way to make this work for Yasmin and her family. He'd make sure that the Palace was in their lives for many years to come. No matter what it cost him to do it.

7

_T_he week went by in a blur of painting and curtain hanging, going out to buy new restaurant fittings, and meeting with people while they installed them. While Lane was being careful to stick to Mano's budget for the renovation, it was becoming increasingly difficult.

When Yasmin would find a print she thought would look good in the foyer, or a potted plant that would work well in the entrance to the kitchen, they'd argue over it at length. There was something addictive about her enthusiasm. But he was the one who'd been charged with seeing this through, to make the right business decisions, and he couldn't let himself get distracted. He'd spoken to the project manager at his own restaurant this morning and he'd indicated everything was ahead of schedule. They could get into the space two weeks early, which would mean everything at the Palace would have to be finished by then, too. It was more important than ever that he keep focused on the endgame here, not let himself be sidetracked.

While Yasmin had said nothing about their kiss at the fabric store, there was constant electricity in the room whenever it was just the two of them together. Tonight they were almost finished sanding back the last wall before they'd paint it in a couple of days' time.

"My God, I'm hungry," Yasmin said as she wiped her hands on her coverall. Her hair was twisted in a high bun, and dust from the sanding made it look gray in places. Despite being the only people around at this time of the night, she dropped her voice to a whisper. "What say we go on a kitchen raid?"

He flicked his wrist and looked at his watch. "At one thirty a.m.?"

"Sure. It's been about six hours since we last ate, and my belly thinks I've excommunicated it."

"I'm okay," he said as he moved the sanding block back and forth. "But you do look a bit tired." Actually, she looked exhausted. Her skin was pale and there were dark smudges under her eyes. Just as well their late nights were nearly over.

"Oh, I guess it must be kinda confusing for your body, eating at this time of night."

He looked down to find her grinning up at him.

"What do you mean?" he asked, pausing his sanding. With Yasmin, he never knew where things would go.

"Well, it's a tricky problem." She cocked her head to one side in an exaggerated movement. "Let me see. If Saturday is ham and mustard on rye ... and Sunday is turkey on a baguette, then because we haven't gone to sleep yet, does that mean we should have half a sandwich each, or should we mix them all together?"

He let out a chuckle at her teasing tone. "I'm not that rigid."

She wiped her hand on an old cloth. "Oh, no? Apart from the food samples that Leo made for the menu changes,

I don't think I've seen you eat anything other than at mealtimes."

He rested his hand on his belly. "When you're in the sort of business I'm in, you can't afford to eat at any old time of the day."

"You're not exactly the Michelin Man."

"I might be if I start eating in the middle of the night."

She licked her lips. "Leo made a halva cake this morning. Every time I shut my eyes I see it with its shiny top. I can just imagine how that crumb texture would taste on my tongue. Mmmmm, it's in the refrigerator and he has some of that thick Greek yogurt that my aunt Mila makes, the one with the crust on the top." She made the low moaning sound in the back of her throat. "And there's lemon syrup …"

"Okay, okay." He held his hands up in surrender. She could pretty much ask him anything while making that sound in her throat and he'd agree.

She threw down the cloth and jumped to her feet, and he followed her into the kitchen. When she switched the light on, everything was suddenly awash with a stark white light, and it caught the shine on her dark hair. Showed the last wisp of gloss on her lips. He swallowed hard, imagining another reason their appetites might have them running for the kitchen at one thirty a.m.

"Let's make a plate and take it back into the restaurant," she said as she opened the door of a refrigerator and began removing the cake and other fixings.

Lane pulled two plates from under a counter, and Yasmin nodded to a drawer where he found spoons. She uncovered the cake and cut two enormous pieces, then spooned over a snowy mountain of yogurt. While she carried the plates back into the restaurant, he followed with the spoons and a couple of paper towels.

"I guess your mom taught you how to make stuff like this," Lane said when Yasmin handed him a plate and then sat on an overstuffed couch.

"Are you forgetting the Pop-Tarts?" Yasmin said as she scooped a large piece of cake on her fork and then dunked it into the pile of yogurt. "I dream about being able to cook things like this, but I'm a sad excuse for a Greek girl. Mom never used to let anyone in the kitchen, and the only things I know how to cook come out of a packet. I think she only did it so we'd come back home at any opportunity to taste her spinach pie or her walnut cookies."

Lane took a bite of the cake. It was good, crumbly, but with a moist, lemony finish. "Why do you think your mom left?"

Yasmin played with the edge of her slice, making a little pile of crumbs, but she'd stopped eating. "I don't really know."

"You haven't asked her?"

She sighed. "Not completely. You don't ask my parents personal questions like that. They still think their job is to protect us from all the bad things in the world. They'll just pretend that this is the new normal, and none of us will make any comment about it."

He chewed slowly. "So what's your take on it? She must've been unhappy."

"I suppose." She let out a long breath. "I think she found it difficult when we all finally left home and were so involved with our own lives that we didn't come back as often as she would've liked. She always used to talk about the Pattersons, how their kids had stayed working for the business and they all lived nearby."

"Why do you think you and your brothers didn't do the same thing?" He was nearly finished with his cake, but Yasmin was still playing with hers. Seeing her so thoughtful and sad tore at him. He wanted to wrap her in a hug, pull her so close that all the worries inside her would become his.

"I guess we knew we'd always feel like kids. If he hadn't been facing this crisis, Dad would never have let me work on the renovation without him. And he still hasn't told Nick and Ari the full story of why Mom is in Greece."

Lane put the plate on the side of the couch and reached out for her hand. "You're doing an amazing job here, you know. I hope it's not too much for you. You're starting to look pretty tired."

She shrugged and then looked over at him, her eyes soft and glossy. "I'm okay." Her voice wobbled. "I don't know what I'll do if Mom doesn't come home, but I don't want her to be unhappy either. If she really is happier in Greece, then I'll support her, but I'm hoping that what we're doing here might be enough to convince her that things can be better."

"You wouldn't consider staying and working here? That might help convince her." He rubbed his thumb over the back of her hand and was pleased when she left it there. He thought of the hotel being nearly completed, of him being called back earlier than expected, and he had the sudden fantasy of commuting between Yasmin and the city. He pushed the ridiculous dream aside.

"I've thought about that, but you know, I've spent so much of my life doing what my parents wanted. They pushed really hard for me to carry on and do my masters, and then my PhD. They wanted their children to have the sort of education and opportunities they never had, and I understood that from an early age. But I can't carry on trying to please them my whole life, or I'll end up being unhappy too. They want me to be one thing and I want to be something completely different."

"And you have your list to complete," he teased and squeezed her hand.

"Exactly." She grinned. "I know it sounds like a bit of a game, but I've really challenged myself with some of those things, and I hope I have the courage to make it through them all."

"I don't doubt you will for a second," he said. And if circumstances were different he'd want to be there to see her achieve them.

It had been a busy week of planning, buying, and organizing at the Palace. After they'd seemed to be getting closer, Lane had reverted to his aloof and distant self, and she missed him. More than she would've predicted. Maybe being out together socially might at least break the ice a little.

Saturday was clear and sunny with a fresh breeze to cool things down. Yasmin had arranged to meet Lane outside the Patterson wedding chapel, and he was running late. People were filing in already and the ushers were standing outside on the steps, waiting for the bride. She was anxious to get inside and see what made the place so successful.

While she waited, she looked around at the courtyard in front of the wedding chapel, back up the sweeping drive to the entranceway and the double wrought iron gates. Guests drove past manicured lawns to the reception center and chapel. The grounds were pristine, with fluffy white roses and green topiaries like lush lollipops, reminding her of the English countryside. There was a large reception area to the right of the chapel, and rose arbors linked cobblestone pathways. An ornate version of the famous *P* and *W* logo for Patterson Weddings entwined with iron roses sat sentry over it all.

Her heart did its usual rumba when she spotted Lane, but this time the beat shifted lower and warm ripples pulsed through her center. She knitted her fingers together behind her back and willed herself to act normally. A gray suit draped perfectly off his toned limbs, and a white shirt was held at the collar with a plain dark tie. His hair was still a little damp, and gold aviator glasses sat across his face. He hadn't seen her yet and she wanted to take a moment to admire the view.

The purple cheongsam dress that had seemed to go so well with her hair this morning was now feeling tight and restrictive. She'd dropped one of her contact lenses down the sink while she was getting ready and hadn't picked up spares, so she'd had to wear her old horn-rimmed glasses. No point in trying to do a decent spy job without the ability to see.

"Hey." Lane drew close and she breathed his freshly showered scent deep. "You look very nice ... and very ... studious."

Yasmin aimed a punch at his arm. "*Buongiorno!* It's my super spy look."

He grinned, then took in the surroundings. "This place is quite something."

She lowered her voice as they moved through the last groups of people and up the chapel steps. "I know. They're a really tight-knit family, the Pattersons. They all work here. Keira, the youngest, does the gardens. Faith, the middle daughter, runs the catering. And I heard that the eldest girl, Erin, has come back to take over the general manager's role from her father. Mom always held them up as the ideal family who lived together and worked together, and they have been successful. Us on the other hand ..."

"Lane!" A clean-cut-looking guy in a charcoal suit stepped forward and shook Lane's hand. There was something familiar about him, but not the girl standing in a blue shift dress beside him.

"Pete. Great to see you here. I thought you were away for summer school." Lane leaned forward and kissed the girl on the cheek. "How are you, Kylie?"

Pete grinned. "I'm off next weekend."

"Pete, this is Yasmin Katsalos," Lane said. "You remember, Nick's little sister. Yasmin, Pete, Nick, and I were in high school and we've worked together on a couple of projects. This is his girlfriend, Kylie."

"Actually, Lane, Kylie's not my girlfriend anymore, she's my fiancée. I proposed last night." Pete rested his hand on Kylie's back.

Lane slapped his friend on the shoulder and kissed Kylie again. "That's fantastic news, you guys."

Pete pulled his fiancée closer to him. "I know it's short notice, but we're having an engagement party Wednesday night, and we'd love it if you two would come. All the old crowd will be there, even your brother, Yasmin, if we can unshackle him from work for a couple of hours." He grinned at her.

She opened her mouth to protest that she wasn't Lane's girlfriend, that she hadn't even been on a date with him, but Lane was too busy congratulating them and asking when the wedding would be.

"I'd have loved to come," Yasmin said, "but I'm working on a project in the evenings. I can give you the night off though, Lane." She turned her gaze to his, but before he could answer, an usher asked them to take their seats.

Once they were inside and had said good-bye to Pete and Kylie, they found a couple of spaces in the middle of the church. The place was filling up with people now and there was an excited buzz. Yasmin couldn't wait to see Genie; she hoped things had worked out okay and the mother of the bride didn't hate her hair. Paul was up front with his groomsmen, looking out into the crowd every now and then and nervously adjusting the collar of his shirt and his cufflinks.

Lane leaned closer and whispered, his breath soft against her neck. "How much would a wedding like this cost?"

She stayed still, didn't turn to look at him, just enjoyed the closeness. "Most people would spend between $30,000 and $50,000 in a place like this."

Lane blew air through his teeth. "God, no wonder the Pattersons are doing so well."

"Yes, but there are a whole lot of expenses too. I don't think you necessarily need to have the full-on luxury touches that the Pattersons offer to make money. I just think you have to be smart about the venue you have, the food, everything. It would be interesting to know how much people spend with us on average. Hey, do you think you could suggest our place when you go to Pete and Kylie's engagement party?"

He angled toward her. "You were invited too."

"Only because they mistook me for your date. I guess they'd think of the Palace since he's friends with Nick, but it still wouldn't hurt for you to mention it."

He was still leaning into her and nodded toward the front. "Ever been in a wedding party?"

This time she did turn to him and grinned. "There's an old movie *27 Dresses*—that could be me, except I was everyone's flower girl in some amazing big Greek weddings. For some reason, the Katsalos family has a ridiculous number of boys, so I was always the go-to girl for the frilly dress and polished shoes look. One time I was even the stand-in flower girl for people I didn't know when their flower girl was sick. I've also been bridesmaid six times to lots of friends and cousins."

Lane whistled softly. "Geez, that's a lot of hair spray and confetti."

She smiled. "How about you?"

"Just once as a best man for my cousin, Rick."

He turned back to the front of the chapel and she took the moment to steal a look at his strong profile. Something had changed in his expression, and she remembered him mentioning marriage once before. "In the car on the way to Constantino's you talked pretty passionately about marriage. What made you believe in it so much if things were so tough for your parents?"

He shrugged. "I've always been determined that I'd make a better go of it than my mom and dad, to one day create a family that would stick together through good times and bad. Your parents were a huge inspiration to me."

She sighed. "I guess you've had to modify your view of them lately."

"Not at all. I'm not naive enough to think that a marriage that has lasted as long as your parents' has doesn't have its stresses and strains, but I fully believe they'll be happy again. It's part of the reason I wanted to help out at the Palace."

A sharp sting began behind Yasmin's nose and for a horrifying second she thought she might cry. "I know Dad loves Mom, and she loves him, but they've just gotten so tied up in their everyday lives. I don't know if they'll find their way back to each other."

"Of course they will," he said firmly. "I don't doubt it for a second."

She blinked away tears and he touched her hand. "What is it?"

"You're such an all-or-nothing guy."

He smiled, and suddenly the full and melodious sound of an organ broke the chatter and people shifted in their seats. Yasmin turned to see Paul's fiancée, Carmel, waiting at the end of the aisle with her father. Whether it was the thought of what her parents were going through, the haunting strains of "Ave Maria" coming from the pipe organ, or the sight of what must be the bride's grandmother dabbing her eyes with a white handkerchief in the front row, something made Yasmin let out a gasp.

Quickly, she covered her mouth, but she couldn't contain the powerful feeling of joy, the overwhelming sense of hope and happiness and *life* on that girl's face, and a tear tracked its way down her cheek.

Her mother had always spoken about the magical power of a wedding. In Greek, Pia would always say that being able to help people make their dreams come true was a gift from God. Sitting in this place with love shining off the walls and hope and happiness in everyone's eyes was almost too much to bear.

"Hey, what is it? What's wrong?" Lane leaned toward her and was whispering in her ear. "Did I upset you, talking about your parents?"

"No. Shush, I just ..." And then her nose began to run and she had to sniff. She pushed her glasses out of the way and dragged her palm across her cheek. With one hand,

Lane reached around and held her close, and with the other he dug into his pocket and drew out a handkerchief. "Here, take this."

She lifted the handkerchief to her nose and blew softly, but the tears still fell and her glasses fogged up. How lucky those two were to have found each other, to be surrounded by friends and family as they expressed their endless love. God, what had *happened* to her? She hadn't cried like this in years. But it felt good.

Suddenly, she realized that Lane wasn't letting go. His arm was still around her shoulders, his broad palm gently stroking the bare skin of her upper arm. She stayed as still as she could, willing him not to let go, and when he held her closer, she let herself relax into him.

What sort of guy still carried around a cotton handkerchief? He was so cute with his lunches and his briefcase and his carefully folded handkerchiefs.

"Okay?" he whispered. "Don't look now, but the flower girl is doing pirouettes. She thinks she's in *Swan Lake*."

She started to smile and then giggled quietly. "It's just beautiful."

They sat huddled together for the entire forty-minute service, Lane holding her close, and his handkerchief pressed into a tight wad in her hand, and she had to try really hard to remember why they couldn't be a couple. They'd worked together so well on the project, hadn't they? And she hadn't thought that was possible in the beginning. Maybe there was a chance that something could develop. Maybe now that he'd let some of his barriers down, he'd start to see how good they could be together.

As soon as the ceremony finished, the tears stopped, but she still lifted the handkerchief to her nose just so she could smell the undeniable, perfect scent of Lane Griffiths.

ane hadn't enjoyed a wedding so much in his life. He and Yasmin had spent the time between the service and reception talking about all the wedding disasters they'd been involved in.

Having been brought up in a wedding hall business, Yasmin had lots of stories, like the Andalusian mother of a groom years ago who'd gotten the idea of a stripper at the bachelor party lost in translation and had organized one for the wedding reception instead. Apparently, the grandmother had needed smelling salts. He'd told her about the time someone really did stand up and say why the bride and groom shouldn't marry, and how the whole congregation had run him off the property.

He sat at their table and took a mouthful of beer as she made her way between tables back to him. Her cheeks were glowing and she made a funny face at him as she indicated with wild arm gestures and exaggerated movements how long the Pattersons' tables were. He couldn't restrain a laugh. The purple of her hair matched her dress and she stood out like the brightest flower in the bunch among all the people in pastel shades. Yes, that was it. When Yasmin was around, everyone else appeared pastel and bland. She had a way about her that brought everything into sharp focus, made every conversation interesting and every moment fun.

When a particularly sexy salsa tune began, she did a few quick dance steps and finally made it to their table.

"Oh. My. God," she said as she leaned down to his ear. "We *have* to put in a bathroom like theirs! It has fresh towels and flowers, and you can try moisturizer and perfume! Here, smell." She thrust her wrist toward him and it was all he could do to stop himself from taking her hand in his and stroking it. He leaned in and breathed deeply, and the scent of a bright summer's day powered through him.

She sat down with a thump. "You've got to admit, the Pattersons do things exceptionally well. Everything's sort of unobtrusive but elegant. The waitstaff are all smart and efficient, and things seem to flow really well. This room with the skylights and the greenery everywhere is gorgeous."

Lane nodded as he looked around the stylishly decorated room. "Yep. It's all done professionally. I do think the Palace trumps them on food, though. You guys have to hang on to Leo. They could make a lot more of their outside setting, too. It's made me think that we could really work on the courtyard at the Palace, perhaps have an outside bar by the bougainvillea. One thing I don't think they have enough of is the personal touch. It feels a bit corporate and sterile. I think we can exploit the fact that the Palace is intimate and friendly."

Yasmin nodded. "Funny that both places are run by families, but I agree with you. Our place feels a lot warmer and more loving." She leaned closer. "See that woman over there, the one who looks like a guest in the soft red dress?

That's Erin Patterson, the daughter who's taken over the running of things. I remember her from school. She doesn't look corporate and sterile."

"No, but it takes a lot more than one or two friendly faces." It suddenly struck him how well the two of them had worked together in the last couple of weeks. They'd overcome some disagreements and had to compromise on a few things, but they'd had the same vision and that's what had made all the difference. She waved her arms as she talked passionately about all the things she still wanted to do, and he wondered if they couldn't overcome the obstacles that were in the way of a relationship too.

"Yasmin, is that you?" A buff-looking guy with his tie undone had pushed one of the chairs aside and now touched her on the arm. Lane only just managed not to react. He had no right to be possessive—she wasn't his girlfriend.

"Bernie." Yasmin turned to Lane and gave him a wide-eyed look that the guy wouldn't be able to see. It was clear she wasn't that pleased to see him, which made his mood perk right up. "Lane, this is Bernie, Genie and Paul's cousin."

"Nice to meet you." Lane stood and held out his hand, but Bernie ignored it and, taking her elbow, pulled Yasmin from her chair. Lane tensed. He wanted to show the guy the door, but it was Yasmin's call.

"How about a boogie, Yas? Don't you and I have unfinished business?" His speech was sloppy and he had that sleepy, unfocused look of someone who'd had way too much to drink. Lane liked him less by the minute.

Yasmin threw Lane a helpless look and he was at her side in a second. "Sorry, Bernie. She's with me and she's promised me this next dance." He bared his teeth in something approximating a smile. "And the one after that."

Bernie looked up at him and his top lip curled. "Are you her boyfriend?"

"No, I'm the guy in charge of her dance card and she's all full up."

Bernie pulled himself taller, but Lane stood his ground.

"Fine then," Genie's cousin said. "There are plenty of less-weird-looking girls to dance with here tonight anyway. You were much better when you were *normal*, Yasmin."

Lane slipped his hand in hers and gently led her away.

"Weddings can bring the worst out in people, too," she said as they made their way through groups of people. "Bernie's not a bad guy; his behavior just gets a bit ugly when he's been drinking."

Her hand was still in his, warm and small, and he didn't want to let go. "That's one thing we haven't discussed." Her hips swayed to the music as they stood away from their table. Bernie had moved to talk to a group of guys, but Lane would keep an eye on him to make sure no other women were propositioned. "Whether we need to upgrade the sound system and the dance floor."

"Couldn't we just treat the whole new floor as a dance floor? No need to make any boundaries. Oh, I love this song," she said as the band played something faster.

He watched her sway, mesmerized, the stud in her nose twinkling as she moved. "How about a dance, then?"

She pushed her glasses up on her nose. "No, it's okay, I'm happy to just listen."

He squeezed her hand and looked down into her face. "Come on, I want to see if you have any rhythm."

$\sim$

Yasmin followed Lane out onto the dance floor, which was writhing with people. It was a fast, fun tune, and still holding hands, they began to move separately to the beat. Any other time, Yasmin would have had a glass or two of champagne to toast the bride and groom so all inhibitions would be subdued. So, why was it then that she still felt so light and free, and ready to dance the night away?

She watched, astounded as Lane moved and grooved in front of her. Now *there* was a surprise. With his conservative and almost suspicious approach to everything, she'd never have picked him to be a good dancer, but he was moving with her, twirling around. The man had rhythm! And somehow it was rubbing off on her.

They were channeled toward the stage, and as they got closer and closer to the source of the music, Yasmin found herself moving faster and faster. Lane's moves were having some magical effect on her, and it was as if she'd always known how to dance. She was gasping for breath when the song finished and a slow ballad started. Seeing other couples move closer into each other's arms, she turned to go back to the table but felt Lane catch her hand again.

"I was only getting started."

She looked into his blue eyes and saw something burning there. He wanted her. She could see it in the way his pupils dilated, in the way he squeezed her hand.

"I'm dying," she said, waving a hand at him. "Let me just get a drink."

"After this one, I promise," he said and pulled her close against his body.

The singer was crooning about a girl who'd watched a guy from afar, a guy who'd never really know her, and how he'd regret it his whole life. Yasmin relaxed and let her body mold into Lane's. His hard chest was firm against her breasts, and her body began to have its own reaction to him. Warmth radiated from each place he touched her and pooled in her belly. He rested his cheek against her hair and she could feel the warmth as he breathed in and out. "You feel nice," she whispered into the fine fabric of his jacket.

"Sorry?" He lifted his head and bent his face closer to her mouth. "What did you say?"

"I said I think this is a gorgeous dance floor and that we should—"

"Funny, it sounded like much fewer words the first time around."

She looked up and he was gazing down at her, his eyes twinkling. "We make a pretty good team, don't you think? We can plan menus and flooring, spend an afternoon in a fabric store and not get bored, and seamlessly blend in on a wedding dance floor while scoping the place out."

"We've worked pretty well together." She smiled up at him. "But we've still got a long way to go."

"I've enjoyed my time with you," Lane said. He pulled her closer so her cheek was nestled against his neck. Each time he spoke, the words reverberated in his chest. "When I first saw you again and you talked about doing all this on your own with not much more than your mindfulness bell and bat-crazy ideas, I wasn't sure if you could pull this off."

She put her palms against his chest and pushed back so she could look up into his eyes. "You thought I was only doing this to fill in time. That I didn't take it seriously?"

"Maybe a little. You've proved me wrong, though." He leaned back so she could really see in his eyes. They were softer somehow. The determined and focused edge that he usually had to his gaze was replaced by a new and beautiful tenderness.

"I'm not looking forward to you leaving and me being

left with everything on my own," she said, glancing away because the thought was too uncomfortable.

He lifted her chin so she was looking directly in his eyes. "I have every faith that whatever you take on in your life, you'll do it with passion and determination, and I know you'll succeed."

And then before she could make any sort of reply, he dipped his chin and placed his lips on hers. Because of the frantic kiss in the fabric store and the way she'd embellished it in her mind since, Yasmin thought she'd know Lane's kisses anywhere. But this was different. It still made her melt inside, but it seemed more insistent, more overwhelming.

Just as quickly as it had started, the kiss was gone, and once again, Lane pulled her close.

"I thought you said you didn't want this to happen," she whispered, still dizzy from his kiss. "That there was too much at stake."

"You're a hard woman to resist, Yasmin Katsalos, but a kiss or two between old friends never hurt anyone, did it?"

"I don't know," she said as she held him close, and let herself move to his rhythm. "I've never kissed an old friend before. But if you're happy with it, maybe we should try it again? "

They kissed in the uber all the way back to the Palace, the only break when they pulled up and got out. When they were out on the pavement, Lane grabbed Yasmin's hand and led her through the gates, and they ran straight into Leo, locking up the restaurant. Boris was eating something from a bowl at the door.

"Kids!" he called out while putting the keys in his pocket.

"Are you back to do more painting? You'll want to get out of those fancy clothes before you do."

Yasmin slipped her hand from Lane's and marched ahead of him. "We've been at that wedding I told you about, Uncle Leo. The one at the Pattersons', but Lane wanted to check that everything was all good for the electricians coming in the morning."

Leo took the keys back out of his pocket as if to open the door again.

"It's okay," Yasmin said hurriedly. "I can let him in and lock up afterward."

"I can make you a coffee," Leo said. "I want to hear all about the food that those sneaky Pattersons are serving. I bet they use instant potato and processed beef." He turned the key in the lock and Yasmin threw a helpless smile back at Lane. "My friend George went to a wedding there and he said he was sure they used peaches with one of the meat dishes. Can you believe it? What next? Barbecued watermelon? Pan-fried mango?"

"Didn't you have roast fig in one of your new dishes?" she said with a grin.

"Pah! A fig is a noble food. A fig goes with everything!"

Lane moved beside Yasmin and gave a theatrical yawn. "I'd love to talk, Leo, but I have quite an early start with the electricians. What say we have a coffee later in the morning and I can tell you all about it."

Leo cocked his head to one side and his eyes narrowed a little. "Okay, but don't stay up too late, you two. We wouldn't want you to lose concentration on the renovation."

Yasmin leaned in and kissed her uncle on the cheek. "You don't need to worry, *Theio*. I have everything under control. Don't I, Lane?"

She threw a cheeky smile at him. *Oh yes, she most certainly did.*

"*Kali nichta*, then," Leo said as he held up a hand and walked to the gates. "I'll see you both in the morning. Well," —he paused for effect—"when Lane gets here from his house."

When they were alone, Lane reached out a hand and stroked the bare skin of her arm. "I've got to tell you," he said as blood thundered through his veins, "when we left the restaurant, I lied when I said your proposal to me was forgotten. The truth is that I've thought about it every day since. Every time you speak, I've imagined kissing your mouth. Every time you move, I imagine holding your body close."

Her lips closed and a blush blossomed on her cheeks. "Lane, you don't have to—"

He leaned in, and whatever she was going to say next was lost under the pressure of his mouth. A hungry fire, a bright flame of need overtook the constant weight of tiredness that he'd carried around for the last week as his lips covered hers. She tasted of coffee and chocolate, and as her breath fanned out across his face he kissed her deeper.

She hooked a hand around his neck and then pulled him closer. "You taste beautiful," she whispered, and when he opened his eyes he noticed for the first time how her inky lashes outlined her big brown eyes perfectly. "I think I need to taste you more."

When she kissed him this time it was hungry, intoxicating. He let one hand track down her body, feeling her close. "I want you, Yasmin," he said, his breath ragged. "Badly. The second I saw you in that coffee shop I couldn't believe you were the same girl I'd known years ago."

"But you were so hesitant," she whispered. "So sure that

it would be a mistake, and I believed you, even though I wanted it to come true."

He touched the creamy skin of her neck. "Did you take me off your list after that?" He held his breath as he waited for her answer.

She pressed her finger over his mouth and then replaced it with her lips. He groaned. This time he brushed her mouth with his tongue and she opened to him, offering but taking as well. He cradled her head in his hand and then took her hand in his.

"Of course I didn't take you off my list," she said against his mouth. "Tall, dark, and way out of my league, I wasn't going to give up on you that easily."

She kissed him again, and when she leaned back to look in his eyes he said, "I'm not out of your league, Yas. I never was."

"But—"

"Tonight I'll be whatever you want me to be." With her hand firmly in his, he led her back to her parents' apartment.

The journey back across the courtyard to the apartment in the dark took far longer than it should have. She wanted him in her bed, but she couldn't get enough of him here and now.

They kissed right outside the restaurant, Lane nearly stumbling over a bush as Yasmin refused to remove her lips from his while he walked backward. Against a whitewashed wall, blind to everything around them, they kissed among the magenta bougainvillea leaves, the light of a waning moon shrouding them in shafts of silver.

"Toast the bridesmaids, toast the bridesmaids!" Monty squawked, when farther on, Lane pulled Yasmin into his arms again and kissed her mouth, her throat, and every bit of skin between. Just when she felt she would drown in him forever, he clasped her hand in his, and finally they hurriedly covered the short distance to the apartment.

Inside, they stopped again on the stairs, Yasmin two steps up so they were eye to eye and lip to lip, losing track of time as one kiss, one caress slid into the next. This ... *he*, was more amazing than she'd imagined.

She smoothed his hair back and looked in his eyes, hardly believing that this wish was finally coming true, as every fiber in her body demanded to be closer, her breasts aching and every scrap of her skin begging to be touched. He smiled back at her, an open, eager smile that let her know he wanted this as much as she did.

At last, and with her hands linked around his neck, Lane lifted her onto his waist and carried her to the bedroom, all the while kissing her lips, her cheeks, her eyelids.

Just inside the door, and still with her arms around his neck, he stopped and she slowly slipped to the floor. The sound of their labored breathing filled the room as the frenzied movements of the last few minutes crashed into an expectant silence. The beat of her pulse rushed at her throat.

Lane tipped his head nearer so their foreheads gently touched. "I want you more than I've wanted anything in my life," he said, his voice low and husky. "More than I thought it was *possible* to want." He cupped her face with both hands and slowly brought his lips down on hers once more.

The taste of him, cool and sweet, seeped into her mouth. While their tongues met, he trailed his hands down the length of her back, then slowly, so slowly and gently, he kissed along the curve of her mouth, and the exquisite beauty of it caused her to moan.

"That moan has been driving me crazy for two weeks," he whispered in her ear.

She laughed and turned her face to look into his eyes. "What moan?"

He threaded a hand through her hair and she tilted her cheek to rest it in his palm.

"It's more than a moan, it's a saucy, sexy noise that sounds as though you're having the most intense experience of your life." He trailed a finger down her cheek. "And for two whole weeks I've wanted to make you feel that way."

She ran her hands over his shoulders, feeling the strong shape of his muscles beneath, letting her palms trace the fine hairs on his arms.

"And for two weeks I've been anticipating doing this." With both hands on his back, she pulled him closer until his chest was molded to hers. His breath loud and shallow, he claimed her mouth once more, and giddy, she kissed him back, thrilled at the power of his touch, the desperation in his movements. The locked-down desire of the last two weeks spilled over and it was all she'd imagined, his reaction—all she'd dreamed.

Lane trailed his hands along the length of her silky dress, swiftly and deftly, and she ached for him to reach the skin beneath. In turn, she pushed his jacket over his shoulders, then tugged hard at his cotton shirt, releasing it from the waistband of his pants, and sighed as her palms smoothed the expanse of his back. Each stroke against his skin warmed her fingertips, the firmness of his body a promise of what the rest of him would reveal.

He groaned in her ear, then with his hands behind her, unzipped her dress, and she let it fall to the floor.

He dropped to one knee and, holding her close, kissed across the quivering plane of her stomach. She threw her head back and rested her hands in his hair. Each time he pressed lips to her flesh, each time his tongue trailed a new line across her skin, scorching sparks radiated through her veins.

When the torture became too much, she guided his head higher and he stood, reached around, and unclipped her bra.

"You're beautiful," he whispered, and the sincerity in his voice radiated warm beats through her. Her heart soared at his breathtaking smile. This man, this beautiful man whom she trusted more than herself, was melting her from the inside out.

"My God, I want you," he said.

She grabbed the waistband of his pants and pulled him closer.

Lane gasped as she played her hand along the top of his pants before she pulled the shirt up and over his head.

Now, desperate to have all of him, Yasmin steered him toward the bed. The moonlight from the window outlined his naked torso, and she wanted more. "Take off your pants. Quickly."

He undid the pants and flicked them away. "Now you." His voice was a low command.

She kicked off her panties, and as he kissed her neck he pressed her back into the mattress.

Closer. She needed to be closer. Now.

Quickly, she rolled to the side, reached into the bedside drawer, and pulled out a condom in a silver package. "I might like to live in the moment, but I also like to be prepared."

When he was sheathed, she held her breath as he

balanced himself above, then eased himself into her, their gazes locked. Filled with him, she closed her eyes, but his voice was insistent, a low, throaty rumble. "Look at me, Yasmin."

The deep softness on his face pulled at her heart, and he kissed her again. As he drove deeper, every sensation was magnified, electrified. She concentrated on each piece of bliss swirling through her.

Lane. This was Lane, the man who already owned a piece of her heart and was stealing more of it with each passing second. When his breath came quicker, she held him tight, so tight, as wave after wave pounded every inch of her body. Finally, he let out a rasping moan. Spent, he fell forward onto her chest, burying his face in her neck as his breathing subsided.

She pressed into his body, his racing heart so close to her own. She reveled in the exquisite moment and the sublime beauty of what they'd just done.

9

---

*W*hen Lane woke, it took him a moment to work out where he was. Bright sunlight filtered through a gauze curtain at a window and he was spooning someone warm, someone who was making soft breathing noises in her sleep. He sighed happily and smiled, something moving in his chest as if settling into place.

Yasmin fitted him perfectly. The smile only grew wider when he thought back to last night, and how minutes had dissolved into hours while they were wrapped in each other's arms late into the night.

His gaze drifted around the bedroom, with every corner draped in Yasmin's wild clothes. Two weeks ago this would've been the last place he'd imagined waking up, but two weeks ago he hadn't been drawn into the colorful and crazy world of Yasmin Katsalos. It might have started with the list and her intriguing plan to seduce him, but that had very little to do with why he was waking up here. This was exactly where he needed to be. He could see that now.

Being on Yasmin's list was certainly flattering, but since

he'd come to know her, laughed as they worked side by side, he didn't want their time together to end.

And why should it have to? He was happy, and surely she'd want things to continue. She might have only put him on the list as a fling, but the important point was, she *had* put him on the list. She'd been thinking about them together long before he had. He pulled her closer and nuzzled her neck. Yes, he had a very good feeling about where this was going.

Noises from outside reminded him there was a lot to do today. It was time he was up and putting the final touches on the relaunch this weekend. But he didn't want to move. He stroked the glossy black-and-purple hair that washed over Yasmin's shoulder, and then she stirred and rolled over to look at him.

"Morning," he said, and leaned in and kissed her sweet mouth. She still tasted as intoxicating as she had the night before, and he pulled her closer.

"Ciao," she said, her voice low and husky. "I thought you might have taken off in the middle of the night. I did check on you about three, though, and you were snoring loudly."

He leaned back so he could see her better and narrowed his gaze. "Number one, I don't snore. Number two, why were you up at three a.m. without me? And number three, what sort of men have you entertained in your bed that leave you in the middle of the night?"

She gave him a lopsided grin. "Apparently, seduction of tall, dark men is a little more complicated than I'd planned. I hadn't anticipated that a wedding followed by a night of passion would take so much out of me, and I woke with a terrible headache." She pushed a piece of hair back from his face and batted her eyelashes. "For the record, you do snore, but it's a very refined noise. And in terms of your last question, I'm not in the habit of spur-of-the-moment lovemaking, so I didn't have a lot to go on other than chick flicks and bad first date stories from my friends." She put her hands over her head and stretched like a cat in the sun.

He left his hand resting at her waist as she wriggled. "I've told you before that a certain Greek man taught me how to treat a girl, and while we didn't get down to the specifics of what to do should I be seduced by his daughter, I figured being a gentleman wasn't a difficult thing to do. And besides," he said as he rolled closer again and she relaxed into him, "if I'd left, I would've missed you doing your cat routine in the morning." He tickled her stomach and she chuckled and coiled back into him.

"Actually I'm not feeling the greatest today. What do we still have to do?"

"No days off yet, sorry. The people are coming to put in a new fountain and I want you to make sure it looks right. You can have a day off after the relaunch."

He kissed her on the forehead and then she shifted and propped herself up on her elbow. Her face became more serious. "Lane, I don't have regrets about last night, but I hope it doesn't change things between us. We've got so much still to do before the weekend, and I'd hate it if things got difficult."

He smiled and reached for her hand. "Of course it's changed things between us, but it's definitely not in a bad way, and we don't need to spend too much time analyzing it. As long as we're still committed to the same thing, and that whatever's going on between us doesn't impact that, then I don't see a problem."

She gave him a mischievous grin.

"What?"

"This isn't the sort of reaction I expected from you."

"What did you think I'd do?"

She sighed. "Oh, I don't know. I expected you to take this very seriously and worry about the consequences for your friendship with Nick. I didn't expect you to be as happy and relaxed as you seem to be."

He stroked her face. "I might've reacted that way a couple of weeks ago, but I don't mind admitting that you've had an influence on the way I look at things now. You've become my own little mindfulness bell."

Besides, this felt right, what was between them, and the last thing he wanted to do was throw up reasons they couldn't repeat the experience. Often.

A small frown creased her forehead. "What do you mean?"

Whether it was the warmth of the sun on his back, or the feeling of relaxed calm as he lay here with Yasmin, for the first time in years he felt okay about opening up to another person.

"I've seen the excitement you experience from living in the moment, enjoying things now rather than worrying too much about the future." He let his fingers trail down her hip. "When I first heard that damned mindfulness alert going off I thought it was kooky, but I can now see there are benefits in not thinking about things too hard."

She rested a palm on his cheek and her face broke into a bright smile. "It means so much to hear you say that, but ..." The smile was replaced by a frown. "I guess we should still keep this quiet for now."

He shrugged, and his hand continued its path over the contours of her body. "I don't think it's a big deal, and we're working nights when there's no one around to see us, so it's not going to be an issue yet."

She winced. "You were going to let the electricians in

early. And I'm sure Leo wasn't fooled by our routine last night."

"If Grace and Leo figure anything out, they're too polite to say anything." But he had no problem with their knowing. His fingers caressed her shoulder, and he smiled with contentment. When everyone knew Yasmin was his, he'd walk around ten feet tall.

"And Nick? What do we tell him?"

Lane grimaced. He didn't want to lose Nick's friendship, but he'd explain that he wasn't playing with Yasmin, that he was serious; then surely Nick wouldn't have a problem. Nick knew how much Lane's restaurant project meant to him; he'd understand that if something was happening with Yasmin now then it must be pretty serious. That is, if he could juggle his dream and Yasmin. The thought made the bliss start to dim, so he pushed it away and touched Yasmin's face. "Where's that bell when you need it?"

"Okay, okay." She leaned in and kissed him again, and suddenly, living in the moment, many moments just like this one, was all he could think about.

Lane was halfway to the offices of *Wedding World*—the state's biggest wedding magazine publisher—before he realized he'd left his briefcase at the Palace restaurant. Hopefully Yasmin would still be there to let him in, unless she'd gone out to speak to a new linen company as she'd planned. They'd had a disagreement over which company to use, but he'd finally let her go with her choice. He only hoped she'd choose something functional. He'd been heading to the magazine to discuss an article for the relaunch and wanted to make sure they had all the necessary information before they visited in a couple of days, so he turned his Mercedes around and drove all the way back.

He got to the Palace just in time to see Grace driving away. As they'd be staging the restaurant with the last of the new drapes and tables tomorrow, they'd decided to close the restaurant for tonight so Leo wouldn't be there, either.

He walked across the courtyard, said a quick hello to Monty in his cage, admired the sleek new water feature, and then stopped outside the window of the restaurant. He could see Yasmin inside. He moved to go in, but the sight of her made his heart stall in his chest, so he gave himself another minute to watch her.

Late-afternoon sun was streaming through one of the windows that was yet to have its curtains fitted, and shafts of light hit her hair. She wore a plain white dress and her hair was back in a loose ponytail. She was moving around a long table with bench seats on either side, furniture he'd never seen before, and she was smoothing a white tablecloth on top. Short, squat candles sat at each end of the table, and a bright jumble of flowers in a low vase was in the middle. It looked like something from a movie about long Italian lunches or the home of a family getting together at Christmas.

Before he had a chance to go in to speak to her, his phone rang in his pocket. He stood away from the window and raised it to his ear. "Griffiths."

"Hey bud, how are the bridezillas?" Nick Katsalos said.

"I'm keeping as far away from them as possible." Lane laughed and moved to sit at an outside table. It was the first time they'd talked since he and Yasmin had spent the night together, and dry guilt gnawed at his gut. He wanted to tell Nick what was going on, but he had to choose the right time

—there was a lot riding on this. He wouldn't give Yasmin up, but he was hoping he could keep his best friend, too.

There was a creak over the line as if Nick was leaning back in his chair. "What about the restaurant?"

"We've got no wedding today or tomorrow, but the new decor will be complete for dinner service tomorrow night."

"Everything on track for the relaunch?"

Lane looked up to see Yasmin gesturing at something with her hands, and his heart squeezed. "Yep, things are looking pretty good. I've been checking in regularly with your dad."

"And Yasmin hasn't driven you too crazy yet?"

Of course she had driven him crazy, just not in the way Nick meant. More in an I-can't-keep-my-mind-or-my-hands-off-her kind of way. "Not entirely," he said mildly.

"Good," Nick said, obviously not suspecting anything. "Listen, I've just had a call from Dad. Things are not good over in Greece, although Dad says you might already know that. Mom's started working part time in my uncle's restaurant and she's saying she has no plans to come back. Dad doesn't want to come home without her, but he's worried about things at the Palace."

Boris jumped up beside him at the table and he scratched the cat behind his ear. "Things are fine. Grace has the day-to-day stuff under control, and Yasmin and I are getting set for the relaunch."

"That's the thing." Nick let out a long breath. "I don't know if there will be a relaunch. I suggested to Dad that it could be time to sell. What do you think? You're there on the ground. Do you think we should investigate selling?"

Lane looked back through the window at Yasmin. It was then he noticed she had headphones on, and as she was laying the table with plates and cutlery, he could hear her speaking in Italian, her arms moving as she spoke. It was another thing on that list of hers, and she'd begun greeting him with a *buongiorno* or *come stai* whenever she saw him.

What would this news do to her? She'd grown to love this place again; they'd both worked so hard to get things turned around. He was certain when Nick came here for the relaunch he'd see that too.

"We've got things covered at the moment," he said and stopped as he realized Yasmin had seen him. "Let's run with the relaunch. If nothing else, it'll give the Palace good publicity and get everyone talking about it again. If things are becoming too tough financially I'd like to help out." If he had to buy the place for Yasmin, he would. She was special. He'd give her the world if he could.

"No, it's not that. I can put money in if necessary, it's just that if Mom's not coming home there's no point in trying to prop things up. I just wanted to make sure you were in the loop before I talk to her and we make the final decision."

Lane scrubbed a hand through his hair and looked up in time to see Yasmin waving at him through the window. No, she wasn't waving, she was shooing him away, as if she didn't want him to see what she was doing. He stood, and a grin spread across his face at the beautiful sight of her.

"Have you spoken to Yasmin about it?" Now she was spread-eagled across the window in an exaggerated attempt to keep him from seeing what she'd been doing with the long table, but she was laughing, and now he was chuckling too. He couldn't ever let her lose this place.

"No, and I'd prefer you didn't say anything, either. She seems so positive and happy lately. Mom and Dad are relieved she's back from all her globe-trotting, and they wouldn't want her leaving again before all this is settled."

Lane's blood heated, thinking about what, exactly, was

making her positive and happy. He hoped she'd stay that way for a long time too. Maybe even for the rest of her life ...

He stilled, body tense.

The rest of her life?

He relaxed, fixed his gaze on Yasmin again, and smiled. Yes. One hundred percent yes.

He'd been fighting his attraction to her ever since they'd met again in the café, but now that he'd stopped fighting it, he realized what his heart had probably known for a long time. He wanted Yasmin in his life permanently. She'd told him he was an all-or-nothing guy, and she was right. Now he wanted it all with her. He wanted Yasmin in his bed every night and across the breakfast table every morning. He wanted little babies with glossy black hair, and a big, stable home for them to grow up in surrounded by her noisy, crazy family. He wanted to be the one she laughed with, the one she stretched like a cat with, the one she grew old with out on the porch.

He filled his lungs and smiled. Everything around him suddenly seemed brighter. The glass sparkled in the sun, Boris purred beside him, and even Monty's screeches sounded sweeter. This felt right, more right than anything in his life ever had.

"You still there?" Nick said.

"Yep, I'm still here." What had they been talking about? Telling Yasmin about the possibility of a sale. "Maybe you should tell Yasmin what you're thinking. I'm sure she'd like input into any decisions."

"She'll only worry. I can handle it, and besides, I don't have time to drive up there."

Lane frowned as he thought back to what Yasmin had said about being protected her whole life. "I think you should make time to talk to her. She's strong enough to hear it, Nick, and I think she'll have opinions of her own."

There was silence at the end of the line, and he could imagine his friend rubbing his forehead as he worked his way to a decision.

Suddenly he had a solution. "Listen, are you going to Pete Worthington's engagement party tomorrow night?"

"I should, but I have this deal that I'm working on."

"He invited me, and if I bring Yas we could meet up there for an hour or so, tell her what you know, and then I can bring her back here."

Nick made an indecisive noise. "If you think it's that important."

"I do."

"I'll think about it," Nick replied before they said good-bye.

Lane walked to the restaurant door and opened it. To his surprise, Yasmin met him in the doorway. "You weren't supposed to see! You won't get the full effect until it's all complete. Did you know about this? Did you suspect? Man, I can't get anything past you."

He pulled her into his arms. "Yas, I don't know what you're talking about." He kissed her lips lightly. "I came to ask you if you'd come to Pete and Kylie's engagement party with me tomorrow night."

The more he thought about this plan, the more he liked it. If Yasmin was to be a permanent part of his life, it was time she met his friends. They'd soon be her friends too.

She frowned. "You want me to come? We have so much to finish here and ..."

"Yes, I do. We both need a break, and it'll be nice to get out of the place. It'll only be for an hour or two, and then we can come back and finish things off here. Besides, Nick said he was going to try to make it."

She looked up, surprised. "He did?"

"And I'd like you to meet my other friends as well."

She scanned his face, as if looking for more clues, then shrugged. "Okay."

Satisfied, he stretched his neck to look behind her. "So tell me why you're looking so guilty. What's that monstrosity over there?"

She held her arms wide and did a dramatic, "Nooooo!"

He touched both her arms, pushed them down to her sides, and kissed her square on the lips. "I'm not going to leave here until you tell me what's going on."

She chuckled as he pushed a strand of hair off her face and kissed her earlobe. "That's hardly a deal. I don't want you to stop kissing me, so I'm hardly going to agree to that."

He wrapped his arms around her, then quickly spun her shoulders and dashed into the restaurant to get a closer look at the table.

He slowly turned to see Yasmin biting her lip.

"You think you can persuade me through stealth and trickery?"

She marched over to the table and smoothed out the cloth. "You've got to admit it looks beautiful. And check this out." She lifted the cover to reveal a rustic-looking top. "It'll be perfect for the restaurant crowd as well. Just like a big communal table at a taverna."

He shook his head. "How many times did I say no to the long tables?"

She moved back to him and threw her arms around his neck. "Not enough, obviously." She pressed a kiss to his cheek and then pulled back and fluttered her eyelashes at him. "Don't I get some credit for stealth and persistence?"

"You get points for being sneaky and manipulative."

"We wouldn't have ended up together if I hadn't been all those things."

"True. And that would've been a travesty." He took another look at the table. "I guess it's worth considering."

She stepped away from him and chewed her lip again. "I'm afraid there's not much time to do any considering. I've ordered all the tables and they'll be here tonight. Grace is coming back to dress them all like this."

"You've got to be kidding me," he said, stunned. The media were coming tomorrow. What would they say about such a rustic look?

She looked at him sideways. "No shiitake?"

Under normal circumstances he'd have told her in no uncertain terms to cancel the order, that he was the restaurant expert and that she was a mushroom expert with wild taste in clothing, but there was something about the way she looked at him, something about the excitement and joy in her eyes that made him ... start to laugh. All the fight left him and instead he was happy for no other reason than she was happy.

I'm a goner.

"It'll be perfect," she said, dancing around the table. "It's going to give the Palace an incredible community feel. Thank you so much for agreeing to it."

"A guy hardly has a chance when he's bulldozed into it at every opportunity."

"Oh, Lane, I have such an amazing feeling about this. I really think it's going to make all the difference to Mom. What say we get the photographer to get shots of Saturday night with all the people, the new decor, and all the new food, and we can make it into a little movie for her? Don't you think that would be a great idea?"

He caught her hands and dragged her back close to him. "Sure," he said. "And maybe I should have a quick talk with your dad before Saturday, to see if there's anything else he wants us to do."

"He'd love to hear from you. Just think, Lane, in one more week, the fortunes of the Aegean Palace are going to be turned around and everything will be different."

As she moved back to look at the table, Lane considered the prospect of the Palace being sold out from under them, and he curled his fingers into his palm. Things would be different at the Palace, he was sure of that; he just hoped it was in the way that Yasmin wished for.

10

It had been a tough day. Yasmin loved the new artwork she'd ordered for the foyer; she thought the pieces were lively and exciting. Lane had said they were too loud and modern. The new fountain had sprung a leak and caused the new tiles in the courtyard to begin lifting, and when she'd suggested laying something completely different, Lane had given her a lecture about sticking to budgets and being sensible. Now that they were standing at the entrance to the Bluebird Club, the venue for Pete and Kylie's engagement party, she let herself relax a little.

"Oh, wow," Yasmin said on a long breath, "this place is amazing."

The large double doors opened into a wide atrium, and crowds were standing in clusters while waiters walked among them with hors d'oeuvres. A woman who must have been Peter's or Kylie's mom flitted among groups of older people, beaming to everyone who came in.

Yasmin had known of many of these people when she was younger—most were Nick's friends as well as Lane's—but she'd never really mixed with them. Like Nick, his buddies and their girlfriends were good at both sports and academics. Most had fast-tracked finance or law degrees and were already making serious money in the city. Her friends, on the other hand, were all academics or artists, perpetual college students who'd likely end up in either academia or a commune in India. For a minute she was reminded this was Lane's and Nick's world and that these people really were out of her league. No, not out of her league—she remembered Lane disagreeing with her for saying that—just on a different track in life.

Lane put his arm around her waist to guide her into the room, and her skin responded to his touch beneath the deep green silk of the dress Genie had helped her pick out. Lane looked incredibly handsome in his charcoal suit and shirt, and when he winked her body warmed all over.

When she'd written the fifth entry on her list, she'd never imagined it'd be more than a one-night stand. In fact, she hadn't really thought about what would happen after she'd achieved it. Did she think she'd just end up saying, "Thanks very much, that was pleasant. Close the door on your way out," and move on to the next thing on her list? She hadn't made a plan for how to deal with the possibility of a second or third night with that person, or meeting his friends. Probably because number five was supposed to have been out of her league. She'd never dreamed whoever it was would want a second night with her. But Lane was different. And now she couldn't imagine tonight ending any other way than being snuggled in his arms.

"I'm underdressed," she whispered as she looked across the men and women standing in small groups. The men were in expensive-looking suits and the women were impossibly perfect, with beautifully applied makeup and chic outfits. "Look at all those gorgeous cocktail dresses. I wish

I'd worn something more suitable." The 1950s dress she and Genie had seen in a thrift store window had seemed perfect at the time, with its flared skirt and its belt in the same fabric, and when they'd found a matching bow in a dime store to go in her hair she'd felt invincible. Now she patted her hair and wondered why she'd felt so confident. She wished it was just the two of them, curled up together on the couch back at home, feeding each other halva cake.

Lane leaned in and whispered close to her ear. "You look beautiful. Interesting and unique and very, very sexy."

"But I look too informal," she said as she pulled at the front of her dress to cover her chest.

He grabbed her hand to stop her from pulling and waited until she met his eyes. "I'll be the proudest man in the room with you beside me."

A waiter came toward them with a tray of champagne and orange juice. Lane released her hand and took a glass of champagne for himself and handed the juice to her.

"Maybe this was a mistake," she said and turned to watch more people walking in, air-kissing each person they met.

"Griffiths!" One of the men slapped Lane on the back, and the woman with him leaned in to kiss him on both cheeks. "It's good to see you out from under your rock."

"Don't be silly, Mike," the woman said as she stroked Lane's arm. "We heard you'd sold your restaurants, Lane, and that you're opening the restaurant in the new Prescott Hotel. I know a lot of people who can't wait for that opening, but I bet it means we'll see even less of you from now on."

He smiled, then turned back to Yasmin. "Mike and Rachel, this is Yasmin Katsalos, Nick's sister." He pulled her a little closer and his friends' eyes flicked to Lane with the universal expression of understanding. Yasmin found a polite smile. Guess they weren't keeping their involvement such a secret anymore.

"So what have you been doing to fill in the hours, Lane?" Mike asked.

"I'm working with Yasmin on a renovation at her parents' wedding hall."

"Oh, do you run it?" Mike turned to her, and she had a terrible feeling he was going to quiz her about profit margins and the state of business confidence in Brentwood Bay. Her palms became damp and she smoothed down her skirt. "I guess financial expertise must run in your family." He craned his neck to look over her head, and she took a sip of orange juice to calm her heated face. "Where's that brother of yours?"

"He should be here soon," she said. She hadn't seen Nick since she'd come back from Borneo, so she was looking forward to it. Her father had explained to both her brothers that their mom wanted some time out, but Yasmin wasn't sure if they knew the extent of the Palace's problems. She and Nick had talked on the phone when he was available, but he hadn't been out to the Palace. It wasn't surprising—they'd always had a good relationship, but he was too wrapped up in his own world to make too much time for family. She was surprised that he'd give up his precious time for an engagement party.

Another couple joined them, the woman equally as manicured and beautiful as the first, the man calm and serious. The group talked about people they all knew, promotions and mortgages, baby plans and Caribbean holidays. The second couple issued an invitation to a long weekend in Napa, and the woman teased Lane about the fact that he hadn't hosted the crowd for a dinner party for a while.

A slow-burning heat rose on Yasmin's neck. She'd felt

exhausted the past two days but hadn't wanted to make a big deal of it. Once they got through the relaunch, she'd have time to relax.

"What do you say, Yasmin?" Lane said, turning to her. "How about we have a dinner after the relaunch is over? We've probably picked up enough tips from this project to make it pretty memorable." He nodded to Mike. "Like the party you and Rachel had last summer." Her stomach clenched tight. The group started swapping stories about what had apparently been a legendary night, before moving on to other topics, so she got out of having to answer. Which was good, since she had no idea what she would have said. She and Lane were entertaining guests now? They'd gone from needing to keep their relationship a secret to throwing cozy dinner parties?

She cursed the fact that she couldn't drink. A stiff whiskey or one of those glasses of champagne would hit the spot about now, or having Genie here to pass comment on all the beautiful people. When she went to take a tiny step back from the group, Lane pulled her closer as he continued talking to the guy beside him.

Yasmin looked around at Lane's friends and a sad and sickening realization worked its way into her thoughts. This was the life that Lane fitted into so effortlessly, the life he'd told her he wanted to grow further as he got older. Country clubs and old friends, corporate people and close connections. But this was exactly the sort of life she *didn't* want for herself anymore.

She'd fitted here once, when she'd been Nick's little sister, when she'd been his stand-in date at company functions and graduations—and she'd made up her mind that this wasn't the way she wanted to live. She watched Lane talking in that serious way that he did when he felt strongly about something, and she realized that despite the physical closeness, the intimate connection they'd made in the last twenty-four hours, they were still so very, very different. Suddenly, the room began to spin and she had to will herself to stay upright. Now was not the time to lose her cool. She took long breaths through her nose and concentrated on a bowl of punch on a table.

She was vaguely aware of someone moving toward her from the other side of the room, and then a hand slid around her shoulders.

"Hey." She turned and felt Lane's hand slip from her back. Nick was standing beside her in a perfectly crisp suit, a smile lighting up his olive complexion. He kissed her cheeks, then methodically moved around the circle, kissing the women and shaking hands with the men.

"Where's the girl we saw you with on Saturday night?" Rachel asked. "She seemed nice ... and absolutely stunning."

"She was stunning," Nick said. "But today's Wednesday." The group roared with laughter. "Excuse me, you guys," he said. "I need to talk to my sister."

Nick took Yasmin's elbow and walked her over to a column, away from the celebrating crowd, and turned his back to the group they were just speaking to.

"I wasn't expecting you to make it," Yasmin said, wiping her clammy hands on her dress. "I thought you were pursuing world domination."

He had a hand in one pocket and was regarding her with such a serious look, she began to get worried. "I am busy, but I needed to see you, so I thought I'd kill two birds with one stone. Cost me an arm and a leg for an engagement present, though." She'd never seen him look so intense. His forehead was creased in a frown and his mouth was turned down. "Are you okay? You look really pale."

"I'm fine," she said. "What is it?"

Suddenly his face changed and he leaned back for effect. "What's with the hole in your nose and the carnival hair? Has Mom seen it?"

Yasmin aimed a punch at his arm. "Of course she's seen it. I've FaceTimed her most days. Don't tell me she didn't say anything to you about it. And I saw Dad briefly before he left."

"And he didn't demand you get rid of both immediately?"

When she didn't respond, he gave her a supercilious grin. "Mom did mention being worried that you were going off with some punk rock band. The only way I could calm her down was by reminding her Lane was working on the renovation and that he'd keep an eye on you."

Yasmin looked across to where Lane was hugging another woman who had joined his group. Things had changed between them tonight, but she'd have to wait until after the party to talk to him about that. She turned back to Nick. "So what did you need to see me about?"

His eyes became more serious. "I don't think Mom's coming home."

"What do you mean not coming home? Not ever?" A lump formed in her throat and she had to swallow before she could speak. "She wouldn't do that. Live thousands of miles away from us. And why hasn't Dad told me this?" Her heart ached in her chest. She hadn't considered for a minute that her mother wouldn't ever return. How could they be a family with her mom living in Greece permanently? What would it mean for her father? For the Palace? For all of them?

"I had Dad on the phone in tears."

"Tears?" She shook her head at the impossible image of her father crying, but it was too much to think about. "I FaceTimed him yesterday and he said everything was fine. Tears? Are you sure?"

"Yas, Mom and Dad would rather lie to you than have you hurt. Dad wants me to arrange the sale of the Palace."

Yasmin reeled back as if she'd been punched. "But the Palace is their life. Their American Dream. They worked their fingers to the bone building that place up. All those hours, those weekends, those *years* without a holiday. What was all that sacrifice for? If they sell now while they're struggling, they might not be rewarded for any of that hard work."

Her brother shrugged. "It's just a business, Yas. And not a very profitable one at that."

"Just a business?" Now she could feel fire start to light in her veins. "The Palace is way more than a business, Nick. It's our home, it's our heritage. It's a symbol of what we are as a family, and I, for one, am not about to lose that. God, why did we all move away? Why didn't we see what we had when everything was good?"

Nick rubbed a hand across his chin. "What do you propose we do?"

"You could buy it from them." She clutched his arm as the perfect solution became clear. He was wealthy, very wealthy, and he probably knew all sorts of ways to help the business financially.

He pulled at the collar of his shirt. "As if Dad would let that happen. He'd rather end up bankrupt than feel he was taking charity from one of his kids."

146

She lowered her voice. "You know I don't have enough money to do it. And neither does Ari. What about you running it for a while?"

"Yasmin," he said, touching her arm. "I'm sorry, but I'm far too busy with my own work to take on the Palace."

"But what if it's the three of us? What if you, me, and Ari made a pact to do whatever we can to save it? Lane and I have almost finished with the restaurant renovation and we'll be inviting all the media and having the relaunch. What if after that you and I work together for a few weeks? Try to turn it around ourselves?"

He shrugged and looked back to where a group of his friends was standing. "I don't know, Yas. I'm really busy and I've got no experience in a business like the Palace. Maybe if there were a surefire way to make money on it fast, then I'd think about it. And besides," he said, arching an eyebrow, "don't you have a PhD to finish? Or have you given up on your dreams?"

Give up on her dreams? If anything, working through her list had only made her more committed to spreading her wings, to finding what it was that made her happy. As soon as she finished her bouquet list, she was going to make another one.

"Of course not," she said, waving the idea away with her hand, "but that doesn't mean I think we should give up on the Palace."

He rubbed his chin. "If I say yes, *if* that's the way we decide to go, then one of us needs to go and convince Mom to come home."

"I could do that while you work the business for a couple of weeks, and maybe then we could get Ari in on it too." Her heart swelled. If her brothers helped, they could really make this happen.

Nick snorted. "You know there's no one on earth who's more cynical about weddings than Ari. And can you imagine him and me working together?"

Yasmin sighed, a tiny bit of her enthusiasm leaching away. "Not really, but if it meant we could get the Palace into a position where it was at least competitive, I really think that might be the boost both Mom and Dad need."

"Lane says the relaunch is on Sunday."

"Yes," she said, suddenly feeling as though there was something positive coming out of this, that there was something that she could do to make this whole nightmare better. "Everything's looking good."

"Looks like you and Lane are getting on pretty well." Nick had raised an eyebrow, and Yasmin could feel her hand go to her throat as she stroked her necklace. "Gotta say I'm surprised, since you've never thought much of my friends. I wouldn't have thought he was your type."

She looked over to where Lane stood, and in that instant he caught her eyes and smiled and she could feel her face begin to burn.

"If you are involved, I'm not sure I approve."

Yasmin huffed out a frustrated sigh. She didn't need to have this conversation with Nick; she was sick of being told what to do and how to do it. "You don't get to approve or not of my love life, Nick. See, this is why I don't bring men home. If, and I say *if*, I was seeing someone, it would be between us."

"He's my friend, Yas. I can't imagine you fitting into his lifestyle." He waved his hand toward the crowd. "You wouldn't be happy living a life like this, I know you wouldn't. Have you thought this through?"

"I'd thank you not to make judgments about what's good for me and what isn't." But he was right, wasn't he? Isn't that exactly what she'd been thinking only moments before? Suddenly, she felt dizzy.

"Yas—"

"We should go back," she said, cutting him off.

Nick nodded and they walked toward the group, but before they got there, Yasmin touched Nick's arm and swallowed back the bile in her throat. "I'm going to hold up my end of the bargain and have a fantastic relaunch, but I want you to be ready to come in with something even bigger when that's complete."

"I'll think about it," he said.

Yasmin was quiet when she and Nick rejoined the group. She fingered the butterfly at her throat and although she was making polite conversation with Rachel about new possibilities for the Palace garden, Lane could tell her attention was elsewhere. She'd be worried about the news of her mother not coming home, and if he didn't have to have a conversation with Nick himself—about what was going on between him and Yasmin—they might've been able to go home early. They still had work to do on the shelving at the waitress stations tonight, and they'd need to check on the delivery of those tables. The press were coming at eleven tomorrow and he wanted to be completely prepared. Although it wouldn't be an all-nighter like some of their other days, he wanted a chance to speak to her properly.

He watched the way she nibbled her bottom lip. So much of the time that he'd spent with her she'd been happy and confident, almost fizzing about what she was doing and what she had to look forward to. Now she looked lost— small, alone, and pale. He wanted to reach out and quietly wrap his hand around hers, tell her that he'd do whatever he could to help, but he wouldn't do it until he'd told Nick what was going on. And the sooner he did that, the better.

When he was about to pull Nick away for a quiet word, Rachel asked Yasmin if she'd like to come and look at the tropical plantings on the roof of the club.

"I'm not sure how long I can stay," she said, throwing a meaningful look at Lane. "We have to work on our restaurant relaunch at night and we have a lot to do before the opening."

He reached out and touched her arm. "You go. You might get some good ideas from looking at the Bluebird's plantings. I'm sure your brother and I can talk football garbage for a few minutes."

"Okay, I'll be back soon." She gave him a small smile.

He leaned close and whispered. "Are you okay? We can leave as soon as you come back if you like."

"I'm not feeling the greatest," she said, and turned to follow Rachel up the staircase. She looked like an exotic flower as she climbed each step, with her dark green dress and purple hair, and his chest tightened for all that she must be going through. He couldn't wait to have her in his arms tonight and tell her everything would be okay.

As he turned back to speak, Nick got in first. "Let's talk." With a flick of his head, he indicated that it should be in private. "Wanna tell me what's going on?" he asked as they walked away to a nearby column. He'd turned his back on the others and was regarding Lane with a look he'd never seen before. Defensive and a little unsure.

"Between me and Yasmin?" No point beating around the bush. They'd been friends long enough to know when to cut the crap.

"It's pretty obvious that you've got more than a working

relationship going. I haven't seen you looking at someone in that way since ..." He frowned. "Ever. Girls tell me I'm about as intuitive as a three-toed sloth, but I'd put money on the fact that something's going on between you and my little sister."

Lane slung one hand in a pocket. It was right that Nick should know the truth. It might take some time and effort to convince him that Lane still had Yasmin's best interests at heart, but if they were to stay friends, Nick had to hear this from him first. "Yes, something's going on between us. It's nice and relaxed, and we've both gone into it with our eyes wide open. I really like your sister."

Nick rocked back on his heels, his face unmoving. "So this isn't some little fling?"

Lane held his friend's stare, determined that Nick wouldn't cheapen what he had with Yasmin. "I'm not sure it's your business whatever it is."

Nick lowered his voice further. "She's not exactly your type, is she? And she's clearly going through a weird phase with her hair and her piercing."

Lane took a mouthful of champagne, giving himself a little space so he could make Nick understand what was going on. "No one's ever listened to what she wants, and it's made her feel insecure and uncertain about expressing herself. Yasmin's a lot stronger than anyone gives her credit for. She chose to have a relationship with me. And I chose her back."

"Or is that just what you want to believe? So you don't feel bad about what you're doing?" Nick said, eyes shadowed.

"You've got to admit that you boys and your parents have always been protective of her. Perhaps too much. I under-stand that you wanted to look out for her, but it's affected her ability to make her own relationships. I think she feels free to do that with your parents away, and a whole lot of new possibilities opened to her."

Nick lifted a shoulder, then let it drop. "It's part of our culture. Chivalry hasn't died for us Greeks like it has for some people, and we like to protect our women. Which is what I'd expect you to do. I'm trusting you to watch out for her, man."

Lane shook his head. Before he'd met Yasmin again, he would've been on Nick's side, believing the same line. Now that he knew the person she was deep inside, he wanted her brother to see her the way she really was. Wanted to try to smooth things out between her and her family if he could.

He planted his free hand low on his hip. "The thing is, Yasmin's been working in a highly competitive field with academics and professors, men who appreciate her intelligence and her creativity, and she's come to like that. She's ready to throw off the suffocating expectation of her as a good Greek daughter and sister." Lane met his friend's gaze squarely. "I think it's time your family gave Yasmin a little credit for making her own decisions, Nick. If she's decided that she wants to get to know me better, I think you should respect it."

Nick blinked slowly and moved his jaw from side to side. "I only hope it doesn't end badly. Who am I going to talk to when my sister's left in a crying heap because things didn't work out with you two?"

Lane finished the champagne and put the glass in the potted plant beside him. "You know how much I love your family, right?"

Nick lifted his chin and said nothing. For the first time in their whole friendship Lane wondered if he'd gone too far, if what had happened was too much for their friendship to bear. But he couldn't not say this. What was going on between him and Yasmin was something he'd never experienced before, and he wanted his best friend to understand that.

"I haven't gone into this with the expectation that this is some sort of sleazy fling. In fact, when the situation first presented itself I resisted for the exact reasons you mentioned. And the fact that we are in a relationship right now should give you some idea how much I value her."

Nick snorted. "She was the one who made the first move?"

Lane didn't blink. "The feelings were very mutual."

"Promise me here and now you're not using her," Nick said, his eyes hard.

Lane felt the full force of Nick's glare and returned it. "I'm serious about her, Nick. More serious than I've ever been."

The beginnings of a smile worked at the corners of Nick's mouth. "You know my parents will be pretty pleased that you're dating. It won't really matter what I think when my mother gets wind of it."

Lane nodded slowly, relieved that he finally seemed to be getting through. "I'd prefer we didn't say anything to them right now while they're going through their issues. But when the time comes, I'll tell them my intentions are honorable."

Nick held out his hand and Lane stepped forward and shook it. "You're not in too deep already, are you?"

Lane frowned. "What do you mean?"

"I'm not only worried about *her* being hurt."

A sliver of unease crept into Lane's gut, but he knew Yasmin wouldn't walk out on him now that she'd checked him off her list. What they had was way more than that.

They had a future. Her list had only been about finding herself again, and now she'd found herself with him and what they shared.

It was ironic that the heart he'd thought closed to these sorts of feelings was so wide open. Everything was different with Yasmin; he couldn't imagine not being with her now, couldn't imagine a time when they wouldn't be laughing and kissing and sharing jokes.

Now that Nick knew the truth, there was no stopping this relationship, and now that it was all out in the open, there was no need for anyone to get hurt.

11

*L*ane pulled on the emergency brake and killed the ignition outside the Palace later that night, and Yasmin undid her seat belt. The journey from the Bluebird Club had been mostly filled with discussion about table settings and the press visit tomorrow, but Yasmin had been waiting for Lane to say something about the conversation she'd witnessed between him and Nick when she'd come back from the roof with Rachel. It had been serious but ended with smiles and a handshake, and she had an uneasy feeling the two men had "come to an understanding". About her. As if she were a child.

"Do you still want to come in and check the new tables before tomorrow?" she asked as she rested her hand on the door.

A small frown creased his brow. "Would you like me to? I get the feeling something's bugging you."

"I wouldn't want you to do anything that was going to be a problem for you." That sounded snarky. She hated snarky, and hated that she'd responded in a way that she'd promised herself she wouldn't. Seeing Lane with his group of friends and his life that she'd so conveniently forgotten about when he was here with her caused a sick feeling that was growing by the minute. It wasn't his fault. If it was anyone's fault it was hers, for not thinking about what would happen between them in the longer term.

And that just sounded like a big, fat, cliché. Images of Lane talking and laughing with his friends reeled through her head. They were people who were so unlike her now they may have been aliens teleported from another planet. A relationship with Lane meant becoming part of his world, the same world she'd vowed to leave behind in her search for a new truthfulness. But where did that fit with the growing need to be with him, the deepening feelings she had for him, and the ticking time bomb that was his departure in a matter of weeks?

"I'm sorry, I shouldn't have said that." She scrubbed her hands over her face and then interlaced her fingers in her lap. She'd never felt more tired. "But yes, there are probably a few things bugging me."

"Start with one," Lane said, his voice calm.

"Did you tell Nick about us?"

He undid his seat belt and turned toward her. "Yes. I'm proud to be with you. I don't think we should hide it anymore."

Her stomach dipped. Was this the end of everything? Now that her brother knew about them there would be expectations about how things would work and what should happen next. She smoothed her palms down her skirt and looked straight ahead into the dark night. There would be pressure about what this relationship might be and how it might unfold, and none of that had factored into her silly little wish to seduce a man like Lane. She'd only considered what would be good for her, not him or anyone else.

She nodded. "If you'd given me warning that you were going to tell him tonight, then maybe we could both have worked out what we were going to say to him." *And if you hadn't said anything I could have gone on pretending this was some little fantasy.*

Lane put his hand on her arm, but she didn't turn toward him. She couldn't believe he'd made the decision to tell Nick—something they'd acknowledged was a big deal—without talking to her about it. He'd treated her just like her family would have. Not as an equal partner, who should have a say in the things that affected her. She couldn't live like that anymore.

"I thought you understood my frustration with being protected my whole life, Lane. I thought you understood that the whole reason for me wanting to live my own life now was because for so long I've been suffocated. And yet what do you do when you know my brother's going to be at the party tonight? You decide to tell him without discussing how and what we say to him. You take it all into your own hands and do things the way you want to."

"I think you're missing the point here," he said warily. "I was able to convince him. He's fine with it now."

She twisted in her seat so she could see him more clearly. "No, I think *you're* missing the point. I don't need to have things fixed for me or be looked after, Lane. Not by you or anyone. And it's none of Nick's business what's happening between you and me. Telling him just gives him more reason to tell me what to do."

He regarded her for a moment. "Yasmin, Nick asked what was going on between us and I wanted to tell him the truth. Like it or not, I've been his friend longer than I've been in a relationship with you, and I believed I owed him that courtesy." He speared his fingers through his hair. "Was it only me telling Nick that bothered you? I got the feeling you were upset before that."

She breathed deeply through her nose and kept her eyes fixed on the windshield. "I didn't fit in with those people, Lane."

"What do you mean? They all loved you."

"They don't know anything about me. Their lives are so different from mine. Their goals and their priorities."

"They're just like me," he said. "People looking for solid relationships and a stable life."

A chill swept over Yasmin's skin. "Look, this is not the sort of conversation to have in a car," she said and opened her door. This couldn't be happening. Was Lane just turning into another person who had misplaced expectations of her?

She stepped out onto the pavement and was vaguely aware of a feeling as if all the blood in her head was rushing to her toes. She grabbed hold of the car and heard Lane calling her name.

"Yas, are you okay?" His voice was far away. "Yasmin, what is it?"

She tried to fight an overwhelming feeling of dizziness, but it became too great. And then she let a soft, dark blanket cover her eyes as she slipped beneath it, the heavy sound of her breathing echoing loudly in her ears.

When she came to, Lane was touching her face. The pavement was cold and hard beneath her back. "Hang in there, sweetheart," he said as he pulled his phone from his pocket. "I'm calling an ambulance."

"No," she managed to say, speaking over what felt like a mouth full of cotton wool. "I don't need an ambulance. I'll be fine, please don't call. I know what's wrong. Can you help me inside?"

He lifted her into his arms and carried her through the gates, her bag slung over his shoulder. The security lamps were on and the fairy lights in the old sycamore tree twinkled. She snuggled into his neck as she saw Monty's enclosure in the distance. Feeling caged and restricted like Monty was all in her head. She was free to spread her wings and fly away any time she wanted. Free to finish her bouquet list. The thought didn't give her the same buzz as usual, but that wasn't a surprise given the night she'd had.

"Wait. We need to check the tables."

Lane held her close and then stopped at the bottom of the stairs. "We're not looking at the tables tonight," he said in a low voice.

"But we've only got three days to go. And the press will be here tomorrow."

"We're on target. I'll deal with the press while you rest tomorrow. We're going to make it, Yas. After all our hard work, we're going to make it. I just wish you'd told me you weren't well."

He began to move up the stairs.

"Then we might not have made it."

Once they were inside, he laid her on the couch and put her bag on the floor beside her. She sat up and pushed damp hair from her face as she looked into Lane's eyes. "I should have told you from the start, but I was worried you wouldn't let me work on the project with you. I didn't want to worry Mom or Dad, either."

A frown dug into his forehead and he held her hand. "Tell me what, Yas?"

"I nearly died in Borneo. It's the reason I came back

earlier than expected. It's the reason I've put my studies on hold. Why I wrote my list."

His eyes widened, then he nodded in understanding, so she continued. "I had dengue fever and I'm still recovering. I'm usually fine, but I get tired."

"But why didn't you tell me?" he said, reaching for a bright red throw before gently placing it over her. "I've been pushing you 'til all hours of the night, not letting you have any time off. Why wouldn't you tell me something like this?"

"Because I didn't want to be treated any differently. I wanted to do my share, not be cosseted and sheltered like I've been most of my life. The only person who knew was Genie. She's the only person who understands why I need to be taken seriously."

"I take you seriously."

"Do you?"

"Of course I do, but I'd have thought we were close enough by now that you'd have told me something so huge. It must have been terrible being so sick on the other side of the world." He sat closer and laid a hand on her cheek. "I'm sorry about telling Nick about us, before you were ready, but it's turned out fine."

Boris jumped onto the couch and snuggled into her side. "Thanks for saying sorry," she said, but she knew tonight had changed everything. She slowly stroked the cat, knowing she had to accept what they had for now. "You know that my mom's considering not coming back?"

He squeezed her hand, and for the first time since she'd heard the news about her mom, she felt teary. When Lane drew his face close, then kissed her softly, all the tension from the last few hours melted away. "I'm here for you, Yas. Whether you're sick, or you're dealing with what's happening in your family. I'm here to help you through all of it."

"Thank you," she said, snuggling against him. "I'll be fine. Once the relaunch is over I can rest, and I promised I'd FaceTime with Mom tomorrow morning."

"Will you talk to her about not coming back?"

Yasmin sighed. "No. That's not the way we operate. We pretend everything's fine and don't mention what's really going on."

"Like you not telling them you've been sick?"

"Exactly like that."

"I want you to know that telling Nick about us has changed nothing," he said. "You and I are both consenting adults who like spending time with each other and who happen to make a great team."

Triiiiing!

Boris leaped off the couch and she slapped her hand on her bag. "I'm taking that damned app off my phone. It seemed like such a great idea at the time, but now it's just irritating."

He touched her chin with his fingers and turned her face toward him. "I kinda like it now. It's made me more determined to have what I want in my life. And that's you."

Maybe Nick's knowing hadn't changed things, but had Lane seen how out of her depth she was at the party tonight? Did he understand that what they had right now could never last beyond a summer fling between two friends? Something in her heart told her he didn't.

Lane opened his eyes with a start. He'd been dreaming he was fighting a duel with Nick, and that they'd reached the edge of a cliff and the person who won the next point would have the power to push the other over the edge. All he remembered was looking in Nick's eyes and knowing that he could do it, that if he was challenged long and hard enough, he could push his friend off.

He blinked and focused on a spot on the ceiling as his heart rate returned to normal. Telling Nick about his relationship with Yasmin had been difficult last night, but he knew deep down that no matter which way his friend had reacted, Lane would still be here lying next to Yasmin.

This bed with its colorful quilt and curled iron headboard had become familiar to him now, as had the soft sound of Yasmin's breathing as she slept. He turned his head and her face was only inches from his on the pillow, her eyes closed, lashes soft against her olive skin.

He'd finally gotten her to open up about her illness last night, but she'd made him promise not to treat her any differently now that he knew. She was so fiercely independent and determined to see this through that he'd had to agree with her. Didn't mean he couldn't bring her extra cups of tea and make sure she was eating well.

He lifted his wrist to look at his watch. Quarter past nine. She'd mentioned FaceTiming with her mom at nine, and he'd organized a nine thirty meeting with Grace before the press arrived for a walk-through at ten thirty. He touched a finger to her cheek, and slowly her eyes fluttered open.

"Good morning, sleepy," he whispered. "How are you feeling?"

She murmured, shut her eyes again, and wriggled closer to him. He took a moment to appreciate the feel of her curves against his body before trying again. This time he nuzzled her shoulder, then laid a kiss on the warm skin exposed. "We've slept the morning away and it's nine fifteen. As much as I don't want you going anywhere, you said you needed to speak to your mom."

She gasped and dragged herself upright, pulling the sheet with her so it nearly covered his head. "Yikes! I need to call her before she goes to work. It's one of her saint's days."

She scrambled out of bed, pulling the sheet with her, but he held on to the end closest to him and grinned. "Oh, no you don't."

There was a momentary tug of war and then she let go, laughing, and stood before him, her beautiful body lush in the sunlight. She dragged open a drawer, pulled out underwear, and hurriedly slipped it on. "It's so hard to leave you in there," she said. "You look so lovely and crumply and sleepy. Will you wait there until I've finished talking to Mom? I want to come back and be crumply and sleepy with you."

He propped himself against the headboard. "I'd love to, but we have the press coming in at ten thirty and I have to meet with Grace now, and you have those waitress stations to finish before tomorrow. What say we meet in the restaurant before lunch? We can work through the afternoon and if we get everything finished, tonight I can take you out for dinner. If you're feeling okay, that is."

"That would be lovely, and I'm feeling fine." She grinned, then started searching for something on her nightstand. "Where's my comb? Mom's made so many comments about the color of my hair I don't want her to think I haven't brushed it this morning yet." She lifted her bag from the floor and scrabbled through until she found it. She dropped the bag on the nightstand and then dragged the comb through her hair. How could anyone look so radiant after a night out and sleeping half the morning? Even the little diamond stud in her nose seemed alive as it twinkled in the sunlight.

"Where's your butterfly necklace?" he asked.

"I took it off when I wasn't feeling well last night."

"You should put it on again. It suits you."

As she pulled her dress over her head he watched her wriggle her hips, trying to make the fabric slip down, and he groaned, wishing she were back in bed, pressed close.

Yasmin quickly reached over her shoulder, zipped up the dress, then came and sat on the bed next to him. She tucked one foot underneath her and grabbed his hand. "I should go. I don't want to miss Mom." She winked. "Don't suppose I should tell her who and what kept her waiting." She leaned in and kissed him.

"Say hi to your mom for me. I'd like us to tell her soon, but it would probably be best if we do it when we don't both have bedhead."

He watched her move out of the room, and when she was gone, he lay back on his pillow and sighed in satisfaction as he thought about their future.

He was glad that he'd pushed past his own doubts about beginning a relationship with her. Now that they'd started, he never intended to stop. He'd give them time to settle into the relationship and everyone around them to get used to the idea, then he'd propose. It would have to be somewhere special for his Yasmin—somewhere as unique as she was. He had time to think of the perfect place. He smiled, thinking of her face when he popped the question. And the ring would have to be unique. Maybe an amethyst surrounded by a circle of tiny diamonds?

Grinning, he threw back the covers and knocked the bag from the nightstand, scattering Yasmin's things across the floor. He bent down and gathered them up. Her phone, a book, a makeup purse, and a piece of card covered in Yasmin's flowing script in a small plastic sleeve. He read the title.

So, this is the famous bouquet list.

His eyes scanned down the list to number five. *Seduce a man who's out of your league. Tall, dark, and mysterious. No chickening out!*

His chest pulled tight. Tall, dark, and mysterious? Out of her league? He'd thought *he* was on her list? He'd obviously misunderstood when she'd said it, but she hadn't tried to correct him, either.

He heard her speaking loudly in Greek in the room next door, and the momentary pang that it hadn't been his name written there dissolved. So what if it hadn't been him she'd thought of when she wrote this list? What did it matter? He hadn't been part of her world for ten years when she was ill and wrote out her life goals. That she'd chosen him now was enough; it was everything, and what they had together was probably so much more than even she'd imagined.

He moved to put it back in when he caught sight of number six on her list.

A trip to Rome. He grinned as he imagined them soaking up the color of Italy on a vacation together, indulging in the food, and dancing until their feet ached. And she'd been learning Italian. He'd heard her reciting phrases from her online course as she sat with an earnest look on her face, her headphones in her ears, so she was well on her way with that, too. Maybe their honeymoon could be in Italy. Rome in the spring would be the perfect place to start their life as a married couple.

Number seven, *learn to dance,* was crossed out and he frowned. She certainly didn't need dancing lessons; they'd moved together so well at the wedding. Maybe she'd thought so, too.

He was about to put the list back when he noticed the very last thing and his blood turned to ice. *Find my artist lover in a country far away from here and spend the rest of our lives traveling, tied to nothing and no one.*

His heart thudded in his throat as the world fell away beneath him. At least with number five he fit all the criteria, even if she hadn't mentioned him by name. With the last entry he fit none. In fact, that description was completely opposite to who he was and how he intended to live his life.

She wants to spend the rest of her life with a man who I will never be.

He sat on the edge of the bed, all the while listening to the excited chatter through the wall as she spoke to her mother.

Maybe the list wasn't as important anymore? Maybe now that they'd begun a relationship, she'd changed what her goals were? She'd clearly changed her mind about the dancing.

But, a voice whispered in the dark recesses of his mind. If she'd let him believe he was the man she wanted to seduce, maybe she was keeping other truths from him too.

He pushed down the sick feeling rising in his throat. Yasmin believed in living in the moment, and right now that was with him.

But what if he'd got this all wrong?

Out of my league. He looked at the words on the list and his whole world began to crumble. She'd never intended this to develop into anything. She'd chosen a guy like him *because* they were so completely different, and that was her challenge. The thrill. She'd never seen him as someone she'd be compatible with in the long term. Could that be why she hadn't wanted her family to know? The thought caused bile to rise in his throat.

Two weeks ago he might've agreed with her, but that was before. Before he'd really given in to her, before he'd watched her lying beautiful in sleep as the sun poured in the window. That was before he'd realized that he didn't want this to end, that he loved Yasmin Katsalos and he didn't want to just be a number on her road to happiness.

He stood and dragged on his clothes. There was only one option. He had to find out what she thought *now*, what was in her heart *today*, not what she'd scribbled on a list when she'd just escaped death.

He set his jaw. He'd believed in what they had. Was he the only one?

———————

12

"Got a minute?"

Yasmin turned from the waitress station where she'd been checking on stationery and menu folders.

"Only for you." She smiled and moved over to Lane. It had been only an hour since she was snuggled beside him, but it felt like a lifetime, and it was time she rectified that by falling into his arms again. But as soon as she registered the distant look on his face, she stopped.

He held up the plastic wallet containing her hand-written list. "I read this. To the end."

She breathed a sigh of relief. She'd thought he was going to say one of the VIPs had canceled for Sunday, or that they'd lost another wedding booking. No one had actually seen her list, but what did it matter now? "I know, embarrassing, right?" She brushed her hands on her dress and bent down to straighten one of the white tablecloths covering the new long tables. "It's one thing to actually have a list, another to come right out and tell people about it, but kinda demented to write it down and carry it around in its own little protective cover. I never expected anyone else to read it."

He didn't answer, so she slowly looked over the top of the table. He wasn't smiling; in fact, he wasn't moving at all. The look on his face remained as cool and detached as when he'd first walked in.

"What is it?" she asked as the heat of his gaze began to burn into her skin. "You've always known I had it, and I'm pretty sure I told you what I'd written on it."

He cleared his throat and tossed the plastic on the table. It was a dismissive gesture, so offhand and so unlike him that she took a step closer.

"I see there are a few more things to achieve, like learning Italian and going to Rome. Are those things still a priority?" His eyes were dull, the skin of his jaw tight. "Or have they changed in the last two weeks?"

"Yes, they're still a priority," she said carefully. "When I can make them happen."

He frowned slightly. "Then I guess you've answered my question. You know, I thought I was on the list. I thought that was your whole reason for wanting to seduce me."

"Lane, I—"

"But it's not me at all, is it? It's just someone like me. Someone who fits a predetermined set of features for a space in time. Let me remember correctly." He spoke slowly. "Tall, dark, mysterious, and out of my league."

She frowned in confusion. "But that is you, Lane. You've become that person."

He dismissed her protest with a single flick of his hand. "That wasn't me on your list, Yasmin. That was some sort of cliché, some set of attributes that you could've found in any number of men. I should be glad you met me before Paulo."

Yasmin's chest hollowed. "What does it matter, anyway? I

think what we have right now is much more than a silly number on a list. Why are you so upset?"

He folded his arms and pulled his back straight, and in that instant she had an incredible sense of déjà vu. He looked exactly as he had on the very first day she'd seen him in that tearoom—serious and closed, as if he were an icebreaker slicing a path through anything and anyone who'd see inside his heart.

In the last few weeks she'd watched his spine soften, the laugh lines on his face lengthen, and this flashback to the old Lane was heartbreaking.

"I don't want to be discarded like a toy on a Christmas wish list. I was a plaything for my parents, Yasmin, and I opened up to you about that in a way I never have before." The ice in his eyes melted for a moment and she saw the pain he'd been masking. "I refuse to be treated like that by anyone else in my life. Especially by you."

He thought she was using him? After everything they'd been through together? "What we've had has been beautiful, Lane. Why would you think I was only playing with you?"

He looked straight in her eyes and it was as if he was racing away from her. "Because I'm not the last thing on your bouquet list. I never will be. And you've always known that."

Yasmin's heart tripped in her chest. "What do you mean?"

He recited it as if he'd memorized it for eternity. "'Find my artist lover in a country far away and spend the rest of our lives traveling, tied to nothing and no one.' That's not even remotely like me, is it?" The twist of his mouth was hard, cynical. "In fact I think we can agree that man is about as opposite from me as you could ever get."

Why was he angry? Why had the man who'd carried her inside and held her so tenderly last night turned into the man standing before her? She pinched the bridge of her nose, trying to make sense of what he was saying. "Hang on —you were so reluctant to start anything with me, and now you're angry because you weren't on my list? I didn't realize you wanted anything beyond what we have here."

"Some of us don't have lists of things we'd like to achieve, and people we'd like to conquer. Some of us like to live a life that considers how our actions affect others." His voice was hard, and with his arms still folded against his chest like a shield, animosity radiated from him. "Some of us like to go where our heart is, whether that's what we'd imagined in our path or not. You're the one with the damned mindfulness bell. I'd have expected you of all people to get that."

The weight of her phone was heavy in her pocket and she hoped to God it was switched to silent. Tears were pressing at the back of her eyes, but she wouldn't let them form. She'd hurt him. She hadn't meant to, but she'd hurt this man she cared about so much. She stepped forward to touch him, but his body language screamed at her to stay away.

"I wrote that weeks ago, Lane," she said softly. "And I've changed it since. I crossed out learn to dance because when I danced with you I felt like I didn't need lessons anymore."

He was looking directly in her eyes, and something about his expression sent chills across her skin. "You're telling me you don't want a man who's a free spirit, who travels where the mood takes him and lives with no ties to anything or anyone? Someone creative? Someone exotic, from a faraway land? Are you telling me you'd prefer to spend your time with a man who's boring and serious, who's committed to building a business and providing security for his family? You might have scrubbed out dancing, but the description of your perfect man is still there in black and white. And he's not me."

Unsure of where to put her hands now, she clasped them in front of her. "You're not boring and serious, and I love how committed you've been to all of this. Look what we've achieved here, Lane. We've done this together. Two people who were on completely different trajectories have joined forces to create something that has the potential to pull my family back together."

"But that's the whole point, isn't it? When things are on two different paths, they might cross at some point, but then they're off their separate ways. And you always knew that would happen."

She couldn't get enough air to fill her lungs. Suddenly it was all crystal clear. No, he hadn't understood that they could never work. While she'd been enjoying what she and Lane had in the here and now, he'd calculated something altogether different. Her knees wobbled. She'd been having a fling, and Lane had been starting a life together.

Grace and two people she'd never seen before stood at the restaurant door. "Oh, excuse us," Grace said. The startled look on her face suggested all three had heard everything they'd just said. "We'll just wait outside."

Yasmin lowered her voice. "Can we talk about this privately? The press are here."

"Maybe," he said as he dug a hand in his pocket. "If you can look me in the eye and tell me that you can see a future for us."

She imagined herself back at the Bluebird Club with his successful friends, and then her mind sprinted forward to them fighting over where to send their kids to school and

Lane married to his job so he never saw his wife or children. And him being angry because she wanted to throw their savings away on a trip to Morocco or Gibraltar instead of trading their house in on a bigger place. They'd both be miserable. Why couldn't he see that?

Another thought hit and she felt sick. What if he could see how mismatched they were, but there was another reason he wanted to be with her ...?

"Is this about my family?" she asked, her voice tight. "Is this about you wanting to be a part of my family so much that you're prepared to run headfirst into a long-term commitment with me?"

There were more voices outside.

He shook his head slowly. "You just don't get it, do you?"

"Actually, no, I don't get it." He wanted more from their relationship than she did, that much was obvious, but it still didn't make sense. She took a deep breath and let it out. The only thing that was clear was that she'd hurt him, and herself.

"I guess that's it, then," he said on a humorless laugh.

He twisted as if to walk away, but she reached out and touched him. "I never meant to hurt you, Lane. I just wanted—"

He turned back and gave a sharp nod. "Yes, it's all about what you want, isn't it, Yasmin? You go on and on about how you've been suffocated and sheltered your whole life, but you know what I think happened?" He planted his hands low on his hips. "I think you were spoiled. I think you were led to believe that other people were available for the sole purpose of adding something to your life. You might've talked yourself into believing that your list was about positivity and growth, but I think it was just another excuse for you to justify putting yourself first. It's called selfishness."

Yasmin stepped back as if his words had slapped her. She'd thought he understood her need to live her own sort of life now, not burdened with the expectations of other people, but that's exactly what he was doing to her. "You think I'm selfish? You think that hiding yourself away from the world and pretending your work is everything somehow makes you better than me?" Her body started to tremble. In fact, it seemed the whole world around her was trembling.

His eyes were wide and blazing, but his voice was low. "I told you my deepest secrets, Yasmin. About my parents, about wanting desperately for them to love me when the only thing they wanted was to make things better in their own lives. And now I find you were treating me the exact same way."

She froze.

Oh, God, he's right.

She'd made that stupid list, had wanted to seduce him, without thinking about how it would affect him. She had treated him like a toy, just as he'd accused her of doing. A tear escaped and ran down her cheek, but she ignored it.

"I never said I was anything other than what I showed you," she said, her voice cracking. "I told you that this time was all about me, that for the first time in my life I was putting myself first. I'm not going to apologize for that. I just don't understand why you're so angry!"

"Why am I angry? Because I've fallen in love with you, Yasmin. I've fallen in love with a woman who doesn't want a man like me. Who only ever wanted an illusion, something temporary she could use for her own selfish ends, and now she's ready to go off and find the man who can really make her happy."

All the breath drained from her body and she had to grab hold of the table next to her. "You're in love with me?"

"Well, I loved somebody. I don't know if it was the you from today, or an image that you wanted me to see, or whether it was someone you might change into tomorrow. But yes, I fell in love with the woman who brought life to the world around me, whose very existence filled my heart with joy, and who made me want to stop being sensible and just live each day as fully and with as much fun as she did." He frowned. "Wait, what's the name of that mushroom again?"

She could hardly make her mind turn back to a life that seemed to be a million light years ago. All she wanted was to be back in her bed with Lane, laughing and teasing, touching and whispering, not hurting each other.

She swallowed to make her voice work. "The amethyst deceiver."

"Yes," he said, as if he'd finally found the answer to every question he'd ever had in his life. "When you first told me, I thought it sounded so mysterious and sexy, something that people notice because it stands out in a crowd. And crazily it reminded me of you."

Another tear slipped down her cheek at the harshness in his voice, and she brushed it away.

"But there's a reason it's called a deceiver, isn't there?" Lane said, taking a step closer. "It's because over time it fades and can't be distinguished from all the other fungi, despite early appearances. Turns out that deep down, it's just like all the rest."

He stopped speaking and an empty, terrible silence filled the room.

The weight of Lane's expectation crushed against her chest and she struggled to pull in her next breath. What if she could have it all? What if she could be who Lane wanted her to be and be true to herself at the same time? What if they could maintain this relationship and give each other what they wanted?

"Let's leave here," she said in a rush. "Let's leave behind the pressure of my family's troubles and our history. Let's go travel the world and do what we want when we want to do it. Let's not stifle each other or expect too much. Let's just go where the mood takes us, living in the present—with each other—and see what happens."

Lane let his hands fall open in front of him and for a blissful, perfect second Yasmin thought he was going to step into her arms.

His gaze held hers for one long moment. And then he shook his head. "Are you serious? We can't walk away from this now. There are people counting on us. We've made a commitment. Why can't you see that it's not practical to throw away your studies and flit from place to place? You're not an island, Yasmin. You have standards to live up to and people who depend on you. And I have a dream about to be realized in San Francisco with people depending on me for their livelihood."

He was just the same as everyone else. He made her want to scream with his regimented ways and his belief in doing the right and sensible thing. "You're no better than my family," she said. "I don't need one more person telling me how I should behave and what I should do with my life. I thought you were different, Lane." Tears rushed into her eyes. "Maybe that's all you've ever wanted from me. To be back as part of this family. Well, you're not my family and you never will be."

She may as well have hit him with bullets. His eyes clouded with pain, and she could feel him draw away.

"I'm sorry." Her voice seemed pathetically small. When the words had formed she hadn't considered how harsh and cold they'd sound when they were swirling around the room.

"I don't want sorry." His voice was calm now, and she could see his face slowly transforming back to the Lane she'd met again on that very first day in the tearoom. The serious brow, the determined look, the aura that said *stay away, you'll never get to know the real me*. "I just wish I'd never set eyes on you or your goddamn list." She watched, tears blurring her vision, as he turned and slowly walked out of the restaurant and into the courtyard.

She watched through the window as he marched toward the group of press assembled in the courtyard, and her heart slowly turned to ash. When the sound of his footfalls had faded to nothing, Yasmin reached out for the little plastic cover and, with trembling fingers, pulled out the list inside. How could something so small and innocent, something that had started out so positive and exciting, be the cause of so much heartache?

13

_T_he next afternoon, exhausted from battling the overwhelming emptiness inside her, Yasmin sat alone in the apartment and stared out the window, Boris purring beside her.

She stroked Boris's warm body and thought about the mess she was in. She hadn't seen Lane since he'd confronted her about the list yesterday, and it was killing her. She'd known he'd want space, so had waited as long as she could, then early this morning called to ask if they could talk. There was no answer, just a very formal recorded message from the serious and closed person she'd met in the tearoom a lifetime ago, nothing like the voice of the witty and loving man she'd come to know in the past two weeks.

Suddenly, her phone rang and she dived on it, but when she saw Nick's name on the screen her heart dipped.

"Hey," she said when she'd connected.

"Have you seen it?" Nick said, breathless. He was obviously walking somewhere very quickly.

"Seen what?"

"The first review of the new-look restaurant is out, and it's damning."

Yasmin's heart seized in her chest. "Why? What did they say?"

Nick's voice became harsher as he read from the review. "'The might of the highly successful restaurateur Lane Griffiths seems to have had little impact on the new restaurant at the Aegean Palace. What he was thinking when he installed long, rustic tables for a wedding venue in this millennium can only be guessed at. One must question what impact this might have on his reputation and the flagship restaurant he is about to open in the newest Prescott Hotel.'"

Yasmin's mouth dried. She hadn't considered Lane's reputation being on the line with this renovation. All those times he'd given advice and she'd ignored it. Her throat became thick as she tried to swallow. He'd called her selfish, and that's exactly what she'd been. When he'd given in to her crazy ideas, he'd been conceding so much more than she'd realized. Giving her the gift of choice, of freedom, even though it had come back to bite him.

"Is that it?" she asked.

"No, it gets worse. 'But it was the very public breakdown between the owners' daughter and Griffiths that left the press reeling. In such a tight market, a happy family wedding venue could do without the bickering between its owner and its adviser.'"

"Oh, God, Nick. I'm so sorry." She blew out a long and shaky breath. "Did Lane tell you what happened between us?"

"I haven't spoken to him yet," Nick said quietly, "but I'm guessing things aren't good. I'm really sorry that it hasn't worked out between you and Lane, but right now my focus is to minimize the damage for Mom and Dad."

The emptiness became an uncharted crater in her chest. He was right—it wasn't fair to go into detail about what had happened. He and Lane had been friends for a very long time, and she hoped with all her heart she hadn't destroyed that. "What should we do?"

"I've left a message for Lane and I'm waiting for him to call me back, and as soon as I get off this call from you I'm calling Dad. It's over, Yas. I don't see how we can survive this. The Palace must be sold."

"No." Yasmin dragged a hand through her hair. "This can't be the end. We've worked so hard on this, Nick, and I really thought we'd done something great."

All the hours spent with Lane—planning, arguing, laughing—came rushing back and she couldn't believe it was all for nothing. She missed him. With every part of her she missed his earnestness and his infuriating attention to detail, the way he encouraged her dreams and the way he followed his own. She missed the tender way he touched her and the shine in his eyes when he smiled.

"Everything's ready for the launch on Sunday, so we may as well go through with it," Nick said, "but I'm going to suggest to Dad we put the place on the market by the end of next week."

"I can't believe it's come to this." Her voice caught on the last few words and she dragged in a breath. She wouldn't cry again.

There was silence for a moment and then Nick said, "No one expected you to perform miracles, Yas. The place was in a sad state and you tried your best."

"Do you think Lane will show for the relaunch?" Her voice wavered.

"I'll go over there now and find out. We have nothing to lose by going ahead on Sunday night, with or without him. At least we might get a couple of positive reviews to counter this one. I'll talk to you soon."

Yasmin stood up and walked to the window, the phone still clutched in her hand. She looked out over the courtyard, and as the tears began to fall again, she wondered what she'd done. To the Palace, to her father's hopes and dreams, to her parents' marriage, to Lane's reputation, and to her heart.

On Sunday evening, Yasmin pushed her way through the swinging doors from the kitchen into the restaurant already filling for the relaunch.

She still hadn't spoken to Lane. She'd sent a text to say how sorry she was about the review, and he said he'd see her here at the relaunch. Things were well under way now, but there was still no sign of him.

The place was humming with people. In one corner by the beautiful gold drapes she and Lane had picked out, there was an enormous wedding cake with tiny silver trowels sticking out, and people were encouraged to help themselves. A floral designer was walking around, giving out tiny corsages, and a very regal-looking butler was moving among groups with a silver tray of champagne glasses. Another carried traditional Greek baskets containing Leo's hors d'oeuvres. The long tables she'd fought so hard for and which so maligned by the reviewer were dressed with white linen and sparkling glassware, and everything had a golden glow from the beautifully polished floor. It was all perfect, the reality of the vision she and Lane had worked so hard to create, and yet there was so much missing as well.

Genie was talking to Paulo and his date in one corner, and in another, Rachel and Mike from the Bluebird Club were talking to a photographer. Even her cousin Christo Mantazis, Brentwood Bay's only billionaire, was here with a stunning redhead. There were media and local dignitaries, interested businesspeople and prospective clients, and it should have been an incredible occasion, a night full of positivity and excitement.

Without Lane, it felt flat and pointless.

With the backdrop of a string quartet playing Pachelbel's *Canon in D*, Yasmin looked toward the door and the court-yard beyond, and tears pushed again at the back of her eyes as she wondered for the hundredth time how they had come to this.

Lane knew the answer. He'd warned her that it would end badly, and she hadn't listened, had been too wrapped up in the rush of spending all day and night with him. He'd said there was too much to lose, relationships that would be irretrievably damaged, and history that couldn't be ignored. She'd been too selfish and too interested in what she could gain to listen to any of it.

But none of that helped her find a solution. In the predawn darkness the last two mornings, and with her cheeks damp with tears, she'd hugged the pillow that still carried Lane's scent, and had failed to work out how she could fix this.

Bottom line was that they had completely different visions for their futures. He wanted a family and security in the city, to be working hard for a life of mortgages and private schools, holiday homes, and investments. In turn, she wanted to travel, tied to nothing and nowhere for as long as she wanted. Maybe children someday, maybe not—there were so many decisions about her life she didn't want predestined, and yet ... she wanted to be with Lane just as much. Ultimately, though, the thought of giving up her dreams was nothing compared to the thought of preventing Lane from living his. She could never ask him to give up a life he held on to so strongly.

Nick was the only person who knew what had happened between them, but they hadn't discussed it more since their phone conversation. It was as if keeping it all in her own head would stop it from being real, might somehow prevent the final moments of knowing she and Lane were over.

Suddenly, she looked up and there he was.

He hadn't seen her yet and she stayed frozen to the spot, wanting to savor the look of him, pretend that everything was still the same, that in an instant he'd be striding over here and pulling her into his arms. Her chest ached for all she'd never have.

When his eyes finally landed on hers, he gave a nod then moved toward her, his body rigid.

Every single time he'd walked into the room in the last two weeks, her heart had tapped a tango against her rib cage, and this time was no different. What was different was the ache in her lips, knowing that they'd kissed the last time, the dull emptiness in her hands that wouldn't hold his any more. Her heart broke for the fact that they'd simply met at the wrong stage of their lives. If they'd reconnected when they were studying, when her future consisted of no more or less than the desire to get a great job and marry a good man, then they might have had a shot at a life together.

She willed herself to be strong for the remainder of this night; she wouldn't allow herself to dissolve in front of him or anyone, not after all the hard work they'd done, everything they'd achieved together. This wasn't about her. It had never been.

"Hey." He was standing in front of her in a tuxedo, a bow tie sitting perfectly at his neck, not a hair out of place on his head. Just as together and collected as he always was.

But there was a guarded look in his eyes, as if he were protecting himself, and she wanted to grab his hand, beg him to turn the clock back to early Thursday morning so she could live their last moments of togetherness over and over.

"This looks great," he said. "Can I have a word in private?"

Her jaw ached with the effort to smile, but inside a voice screamed for him to not be so polite. It would be easier if he got angry, raged at her and told her what she'd done to him, at least for one last time let her see inside his beautiful, passionate soul.

"Of course. I wanted to talk to you as well. I'm so sorry about the review."

He shrugged. "It's only one. I've been in this business long enough to know you can't please all the people all of the time."

"Yes, but I hadn't thought about what any of this could do for your reputation."

He nodded toward the French doors. "The courtyard's probably the quietest place while everyone's in here."

She followed him outside, his broad-shouldered profile impressive within the inky suit, and she remembered the way she'd molded herself into that back in her bed, how she'd slipped her arm around his taut stomach and he'd wound his fingers in hers.

She twisted a piece of hair around her finger. "Lane, I'm so sorry about everything."

He sat back on the seat and looked up at her. "Sit down."

She sat next to him, careful not to touch, desperate to have this conversation without disintegrating.

Before she could say anything, he reached into his jacket and pulled out a thick white envelope. "I want you to have this."

"What is it?" she asked as she took it from him.

"I guess it's a bit of an apology, and my way of saying I understand what you need to do with your life."

She let it sit in her lap and looked into his face, searching for what he was thinking. "Lane, you're the last person who should apologize. Throughout our whole relationship you've been honest and straight up, and I've spent my whole time convincing myself that we wouldn't get hurt, that if we didn't think about tomorrow we could focus on how incredible today was."

He shook his head. "It's been your determination to stay true to what you believe in that's convinced me to remain true to what's important to me, too."

"But I was so reckless. With your reputation and that of the Palace. I was so focused on doing what I wanted. And now you want to give me a gift? I don't know what to say." She gulped.

"You don't have to say anything. Just think of it as a thank-you."

Now tears threatened, and she pinched the bridge of her nose. No crying. "A thank-you for what? I'm the one who should thank you for giving up your life in the last few weeks, for putting up with my madness, for making me feel alive again."

"And for filling number five on your list." He grinned.

"And for filling number five on my list." The last of her words wobbled and she struggled to speak again. "These last few weeks have been the most incredible, beautiful weeks of my life and I can't imagine spending my days and nights without you," she said desperately. "How can we fix things?"

He met her gaze with his piercing blue eyes. "I talked to Nick last night, and then I called your father."

She searched his face. "You called Dad in Greece? To talk about the review?"

"No, I told him I didn't think he should sell the Palace. I asked if I could stay on here to ensure that all the changes we've made are embedded and to manage the turnaround that I believe will begin to happen here. He agreed."

Her mouth dried and she frowned. "You'd do that? But you have your dream project starting any day. How could you make it work?"

"The hotel restaurant was my dream project because it was my passion, but now I've found another one. I told your father that spending time here had made me realize that at the heart of what I love about the restaurant business is relationships and people, togetherness and family. I want to help get those things back for the Palace."

"But how could you manage two places at once?"

Grace put her head around the door. "Sorry to interrupt, Lane, but one of the reporters wants to speak to you."

He stood up. "I should get back."

She stood and touched his arm, her head spinning from all he'd just told her. She held up the envelope. "You still haven't told me what you're thanking me for."

He took a deep breath and then paused before looking her directly in the eye. "You made me remember. Remember how fun life can be, how it's important not to take things too seriously, but at the same time not to lose sight of what's important. I've loved every second I've spent with you, Yasmin, but now it's time for you to finish what you've started, set yourself new goals to meet. Just know that I'll never forget you. Oh, and so there's no confusion, I still intend to stay close to your family, to Nick and your parents, and I hope that won't be a problem for you."

Lightning fast, he drew her to him and kissed her hard and long. She heard him pull in a sharp breath, and then he let her go and walked back into the restaurant.

Quaking all over, Yasmin looked down at the envelope in her hand and stroked it with a shaking fingertip. She could feel her bottom lip start to wobble as she hooked a finger under the flap of the envelope, then lifted out a cardboard wallet inside. Stamped on the front was the name of a European airline. Frowning, she flicked it open and then her heart stood still. A ticket. From San Francisco to Rome.

Without doubt, this was the most perfect gift she'd ever received, and it broke her heart in two.

Yasmin spent the next hour talking to guests, posing for photographs, and trying to stop the unrelenting ache in her chest. Every few minutes she found herself looking for Lane, straining to hear his laugh and to watch the intense and focused way he spoke to people about the renovation.

How could she leave here? How could she leave him, knowing the way he made her feel, knowing there was so much she wanted to do with him, experience with him? Trying to imagine traveling to Italy without him was impossible; contemplating never waking up beside him again, unthinkable.

When dinner was over, Grace welcomed everyone to the Palace and gave a short introduction. "And through this whole process," she was saying, "the Aegean Palace has been incredibly fortunate to have the superb skills of leading restaurateur Lane Griffiths to spearhead this rebirth."

There was a deafening round of applause as Lane took the microphone from Grace and waited for quiet. "Ladies and gentlemen," he said in that low, smooth voice Yasmin had come to know like the beat of her own heart. "I'd like to welcome you all here to the relaunch of the brand-new Aegean Palace."

There was murmuring, and a few people broke into more applause. He looked so handsome in his tuxedo, and he spoke with such confidence and certainty that it brought more tears to Yasmin's eyes. What if she'd never gotten sick? What if she hadn't been faced with the possibility of never seeing her dreams come true? Maybe then she wouldn't have this battle raging inside her—one half of her heart desperate to be true to her dreams, the other lost to Lane Griffiths. She thought of the airline ticket in its envelope, carefully tucked into her handbag, and she knew it was a symbol of the different lives she and Lane wanted to lead.

"Many of you will know me from my chain of restaurants in the city, and the experience I've had in hospitality management, but what you may not know is that my love for food and entertaining people began right in this very restaurant," Lane said.

He held his hands wide and memories of lying wrapped in those arms, against his firm chest, stung. She'd never imagined him speaking in public like this, talking of his younger self and wearing his heart on his sleeve.

"It's true that I learned to cook by watching Pia and Mano Katsalos preparing souvla for wedding receptions and baking Greek sweets for dessert, but that's not the greatest thing I learned from them. Ladies and gentlemen, Pia and Mano Katsalos taught me about the power of a community, about the love and acceptance in a family that help an individual grow and prosper. Spending my impressionable years in the Aegean Palace gave me hope for families of the future, and an unbending belief that love can have the power to overcome anything. In my restaurants I've always tried to bring back that feeling of family and togetherness that I experienced every time I stepped through these doors, and now we've made sure that's the real focus of the Aegean Palace for new generations."

As he spoke, the lump in Yasmin's throat became harder. Was this the same aloof, detached man she'd met again only a few weeks ago? The audience was hanging on his every word. Nick and Grace were beaming in a corner. Leo was wiping his eyes with his apron, and when Genie caught Yasmin's eye she did a dramatic two-fisted bump above her heart. Yes, Lane was having that effect on everyone.

"In a world of competition and the constant drive for success, it can be easy to lose sight of those things," Lane said. "But in the new-look Aegean Palace, we want to celebrate community, embrace family, and acknowledge the importance of those two things in all our lives. To that end we've completely redecorated." For the first time in his speech he looked up and when his eyes found hers, a slow smile spread across his face. "We've put in long tables so that people can mix and mingle more readily. We've designed a whole new menu that celebrates the colorful Greek heritage of so many of our clientele, but which is also modern and fresh, and something that will appeal to every couple, Greek or otherwise. A wedding is a time in a couple's lives when they get to share the person they love most in the world with the people who have always been there for them."

Lane's gaze held Yasmin's, and although his lips kept moving, his words were drowned out by the beat of blood in her ears. Her family, this place, the renovation—they'd all had such a profound effect on him. She could see it in his eyes, could feel it deep in her heart. And he'd changed her view of herself, too. She'd come to see this place and her family as something precious and worth fighting for, her history and heritage something to cherish. But what if her drive to do things her way had cost Lane his reputation and the Palace its very existence? Above everything, what would her life be worth if she got on a plane and flew to the other side of the world without Lane?

Wrenching her gaze from his, she looked desperately for the door. She couldn't listen anymore, had to have air. She ran across the back of the room and out to the courtyard, pulling in ragged breaths as Lane's smooth voice played in her ears.

Her vision was blinded with tears as she stumbled away from the restaurant and was only dimly aware of the sound of the door closing. He'd come to get her. He'd come to tell her he was ready to run off into the sunset and claim their happily ever after. When she turned around, she realized it was Nick.

"Yas, are you okay?"

"Not really," she choked. She'd tell him about how sick she'd really been when tonight was over, but she wanted him to understand how she was feeling right now. "I think I've ruined everything."

"You mean between you and Lane? I saw you talking earlier and I'd assumed you'd sorted some things out, but I can tell things aren't right."

Yasmin dragged a hand across her cheek. "He gave me a ticket to Italy. He bought me a one-way trip so I could live my dreams and I've never been more lost in my life. And what have I done to the Palace?"

She hiccupped on the last word, and Nick laid a hand on her shoulder. "What have you done? You've breathed new life into this place, Yas."

She frowned. "But the review—"

"You guys have done a terrific job here, way beyond my expectations, and Dad's too. Lane says he's talked to some of the other press who were here that day and they raved about everything being so fresh and new."

"But the tables—"

Nick touched her shoulder so she had to turn back toward the restaurant. "See how incredible it looks? See how everyone's enjoying themselves? You've done all the right things here, Yas, and now Lane's going to stay on and see things through."

Yasmin looked into her brother's face. "But how can he do two jobs at once? That hotel project means everything to him."

Nick shrugged. "Apparently not anymore. He's going to give up the restaurant and concentrate all his energies here."

Yasmin gasped. Not only had Lane honored her list and her dreams, but in agreeing to stay on at the Palace, he'd had the strength to alter the things he wanted to do in his own life, for the simple reason that it would bring happiness to the lives of others.

She looked back inside the brightly lit restaurant. Nick was right; it was full of people celebrating life, and she realized what Lane had done for her. He'd allowed her to be who she wanted to be—no strings, no expectations, and never in her whole life had she felt more cherished, more honored, and more loved.

And it suddenly made everything clear. There was something she needed to do for him, too.

～

Later in the evening, Lane stood in front of the audience, though his chest remained as hollow as it had been for days.

In so many ways, this night had turned out exactly as he wanted: new decor, fresh menu, and an energized crowd of important and influential people, but in one all-encompassing way, tonight was the hardest of his life.

His heart told him he'd lost Yasmin, but his head knew better.

She was never mine to lose.

And his head also told him that things could have turned out much worse—his relationship with Nick could have been damaged, and more than just the one reviewer could have taken a shot at him—but none of that counted for anything when the woman he loved with every part of himself wanted something different.

He cleared his throat, ready to wrap the evening festivities up. One last time he looked for Yasmin or Nick. He'd left them outside in the courtyard for more than an hour, but he couldn't hold off any longer. "I trust you enjoyed Leo's food. I'm sure you'll agree that he's a culinary genius." There were comments and whistles, and Lane noticed Yasmin finally step in from the courtyard with Nick. Maybe they'd been discussing the date she'd leave here to go off on her great adventure. Of course she'd never be completely gone from his world; he fully intended to be part of her parents' and

Nick's lives for years to come, but he knew he'd always burn for her.

"There is, of course, dessert," he said, trying to focus on the purpose of being here, "and I don't want to keep you from that, but there is just one more announcement I'd like to make before we bury ourselves in baklava."

"Wait!"

The whole room turned to see Yasmin walking quickly from the back of the room. "I'd like to say a few words first."

The crowd parted and she moved toward him, her white dress hugging the beautiful shape of her that had become so familiar. The purple streak in her hair shone and a smile covered her perfect face.

What is she doing?

"Just give us a couple of minutes," he said to the crowd.

"No," she said as she made it to the stage and drew up beside him. "I want everyone to hear this."

The crowd suddenly stilled and Lane managed to catch her eye. "Are you okay?" he whispered. "Are you feeling sick?"

"I've never felt more alive in my life," she said. She pushed a purple strand of hair over her shoulder, and the stud in her nose twinkled under the new restaurant lights as she stepped in front of the microphone. "Ladies and gentleman, my name is Yasmin Katsalos, and like Lane, I've spent an awful lot of time in this place and it holds very powerful memories for me."

She reached out and grabbed his hand, then squeezed. Her palm was damp and her cheeks were red, just like they were when she'd blushed that very first day he'd seen her again, and his whole body ached with the need to be close to her. When he stepped back to give her room, she held his hand more firmly and pulled him to stand alongside her.

"But I have to tell you that none of those days compares to what I'm feeling right now. Hearing Lane speak about the values of the Palace, how in this relaunch we're also rebooting to a time of strong communities and connected families, it's made me realize that in my pursuit of things that make me feel alive, there's nothing that makes me happier than the joy of the people around me."

Yasmin turned and gazed into Lane's face, her brown eyes sparkling with tears. "The other day, I said a terrible thing. I told Lane he'd never be a part of this family. Nothing could be further from the truth, both because I want nothing more than that to be true and because he always has been.

"Recently, I had a brush with death in Borneo, and after I found out I was going to survive, I made a list of all the things I wanted to do with my life: my bouquet list. And in a week or so, I'm going to take a trip to Rome, to fulfill a dream I've always had, and I'm hoping I can fulfill the very newest thing on my list—take Lane to Rome. I'm hoping with all my heart that the man I love will come with me so we can share the joy together."

The sound in Lane's ears became muffled and all he could hear were the last words Yasmin had just spoken. She loved him? Wanted to travel with him? The hole in his chest became filled with his wildly beating heart.

"And then in a month or two I'm hoping we can return to Brentwood Bay to start working through his own list of dreams."

"What are you saying?" Lane whispered. "I've agreed to run things for your dad. You need to go off and not feel tied down by me or anyone."

"Sweetheart, don't you see," she said, turning toward him, her face shining. "All I was looking for in my list was a chance to feel alive, to feel as though my time on this earth was worth something, but you've made me realize that nothing will be worth anything if I'm not with you. There's one other entry on my list that I still need to fulfill, and that's to follow my heart and not my head. I love you, Lane, and I want to be with you. Always."

She stepped forward and threw her arms around his neck. "I've talked to Nick and he's agreed to step in while we take our trip to Rome, and then I want us to come back here and build a new list, of all the things we want to do in our lives. Together."

There might have been cheering, a band might have been playing in the background, but all Lane could hear were the words of the woman he loved telling him she wanted to be with him. He took her in his arms and kissed her perfect mouth.

"I just want what you want," Yasmin said when she finally lifted her lips from his and looked up into his eyes. "That's the thing that's going to make me happy from now on. You're always going to be my number ten."

He touched her cheek. "We'll work it out. We know we can work together, we've proven we can laugh 'til dawn, and we'll have the love of your family behind us."

"*Our* family," she said, and his heart soared.

"Is this just a publicity stunt?" someone yelled.

"What kind of idiot are you?" Genie called back. "Can't you see how much these two love each other? When a woman declares her love for a man in public and then he kisses her like that, there's your real happy ending."

"I knew it!" Leo shouted. "Those kids never had me fooled. I saw they loved each other from the very start!"

"You're sure?" Lane asked when Yasmin laughed and turned back to him. "Is this really what you want?"

She touched his cheek and the look on her face gave him the answer he wanted. "Lane Griffiths, I want a whole lot more than this. I want a wedding and babies and a honeymoon in Gibraltar. Where's a piece of paper? I need to write another list."

~

Thank you for reading *Making the Love List*. I hope you love Yasmin and Lane as much as I do. Find out what's happening now at the Aegean Palace in the second book in the series *Winning the Wedding War - Nick's story* available at all online book retailers in ebook and print, or ask for it at your local book store or library.

And to find out about new books, sign up for my news-letter **here or email** barb@barbaradeleo.com. When you sign up I'll send you the FREE prequel to this series *Waiting on Forever - Alex's story*!

If you love the people of Brentwood Bay, meet more of them in the *Breaking Through* series! You can find Book 1 *Bad Reputations* as an e book on Amazon, or ask for it at your local book store or library.

I hugely appreciate your help in spreading the word about my books, including telling a friend. Reviews help readers find books! Please review *Making the Love List* here or on your favorite site.

Turn the page for an excerpt from *Winning the Wedding War*.

Two rival families. Two competing wedding venues. One wedding of the season.

Nick Katsalos has a foolproof plan to save his parents' floundering wedding venue. The last thing he expects is for Erin Patterson, the captivating daughter of his parents' biggest rival, to waltz in and charm the client who could finally get the family business back on track. Nick would be furious—if only he could stop thinking about her.

When Erin and Nick enter into a wager to determine who will win the contract she prepares for the worst ... and is surprised by the glimpses of warmth she sees in the man behind the numbers. But Erin isn't about to forfeit what could be the biggest wedding of the decade to a man as cold as Nick. Especially since securing it means she could finally prove to her father she's just as capable of handling the family business as him.

But as the competition heats up, Erin and Nick must decide what's more important—winning or love.

You can read the first chapter of *Winning the Wedding War* on the next few pages.

You can buy *Winning the Wedding War* here or ask for it at your book store or local library.

WINNING THE WEDDING WAR

CHAPTER ONE

*A*s he strode the well-tended path to Congressman Williams's office in Brentwood Bay, Summerville County, Nick Katsalos considered executing a side heel click like the ones he'd seen in cartoons as a kid.

Of course he'd never be seen dead committing a random act of emotion or public display of crazy, but it had been years since he'd experienced such a high in this sleepy little town, and it felt damn good. He reconsidered and did an internal fist pump instead.

Finally, after weeks of uncertainty, he'd created a fool-proof plan to rescue his parents' wedding hall business. As soon as the contract for the wedding of Congressman Williams's daughter was signed, he'd leave the bridezillas and strung out mothers at the Aegean Palace in the hands of the company's highly efficient wedding planner, his mother would come to her senses and return home from Greece, and he could get back to his real job and the predictable rush of the city. His family's life could then return to the noisy, crazy chaos they liked to call normal, and the gnawing guilt he'd always carried for their troubles would finally be buried for good.

He took the stairs two at a time and arrived at reception with an extra spring in his step, still a little surprised to have received the invitation to sign the contract so soon. While the wedding planner was fully capable of doing all this on her own, he wanted to make sure that nothing could go wrong. A month in Brentwood Bay was a month of his life he'd never get back, but he didn't want to return to pick up any pieces.

"May I help you?" A young woman with fiery red hair regarded him from behind the desk.

"Nick Katsalos. Here to see Congressman Williams."

She shifted her gaze to a computer screen, then gave him a beaming smile. "Oh yes. He shouldn't be long." She nodded toward the lobby on her right. "Please, take a seat."

He turned and stopped still. A woman was already seated in the middle of the room, and the sight of her caused the air in his lungs to evaporate.

Her back was ruler straight as she perched on the edge of the plush chair with her head tilted. Dark blond hair was caught in a sleek ponytail low on her neck, and diamond earrings winked from her lobes. Deep pink lips were curved in a half smile as if she held all the secrets of the world, and he had an overpowering urge to know every last one of them.

She turned and gazed back at him with eyes the color of the ocean in summer, then she blinked and quickly looked away.

Clearing his throat, he strode forward and took the neighboring seat. The whole of her, from the precisely cut, pale-blue business suit, to the cream heels accentuating a pair of tanned calves tucked neatly to the side, was perfect.

"Here to see the congressman?" He picked up a yachting magazine and flicked through it with feigned interest. "Looks like he's running late."

"Yes."

He'd expected her voice to be breathy and light, but it was firm and direct, and he wanted to hear it again. "Been waiting long?"

He turned, ready to ask why she was here, but saw she was intently interested in the print on the opposite wall. "You like Rockwell?" he asked, noting her flawless skin and the confident angle of her chin.

She moistened her lips and a bolt of bare-knuckle desire pulled through him. "Oh, is that who it's by?" she asked. "I don't know anything about art." She waved her hand in the air, and it reminded him of the wing of an exotic bird. "I was just admiring the way he's created the people. They seem so real."

For just a moment she turned to him, then flicked her eyes back to the print, a soft blush tinting her cheeks. There was something oddly familiar about her, but he couldn't put his finger on it. Was she the sister of an old friend? Someone he'd dated in high school? No, he'd never have forgotten someone like her.

"The shoppers," she continued, "the businessman and the errand boy reading the news of the stock market crash together. You can feel their emotions. It's quite powerful, don't you think?"

"A picture with emotions?" he asked, trying to hide his amusement. "You know there's a mistake in it."

She turned back and this time held his stare, her eyes sparking. "Sorry?"

"There's a mistake. The errand boy has three legs."

A small frown creased her forehead, and then she

laughed, softly at first and then loudly as if he'd told her the funniest thing she'd ever heard. "What do you mean, a mistake?"

"There is." He nodded toward the picture. "You can see how the boy's legs run straight up and down at the back, right?"

She rolled her lips together, and despite the fact he should be looking at the picture, too, he couldn't pull his eyes from her. "Yes."

He leaned forward so their bodies were in line and the air crackled. "But his hands are also resting on a bent knee at the front. Two legs at the back, one at the front. That's gotta be uncomfortable."

She stood up, walked to the wall, and peered closely, her back still straight, but now he could see the curve of her hips and the smooth-as-silk skin at the back of her neck. "No, you're wrong. It's just the way his apron's falling across his knee."

"Uh-uh. Three legs."

"How do you know?" she said, twisting back to him. She sounded slightly annoyed, as if he'd just told her Bambi was a delinquent fawn that didn't really care what happened to its mommy. "Are you an art expert?"

He shrugged. "Call it a hobby. A public service." Her frown was darkening, so he continued. "TV shows, movies, books, you'd be surprised how many are full of continuity errors."

She blinked and then there was that secret smile again as if she knew his innermost thoughts. Or as if he amused her. And she let out another laugh. "You mean you find these sorts of things on a regular basis? And go around destroying people's enjoyment by telling them about it?"

He leaned back in his chair. "I only ever see movies by accident—over someone's shoulder on a plane, for example. And you'd only catch me in an art gallery if I needed to use the bathroom, but if there's a mistake, I see it as my duty to expose it."

She sat beside him again and looked at him as if he were something on the bottom of her shoe. This was the point where most people would agree with him or change the subject. She pushed on. "Like when? In which movies?"

He threw a glance at his watch. The appointment was for 3:30. It was now 3:32. He looked back at her and smiled. "I can see you're one of those people whose dreams would be crushed if I mentioned it."

She kept her crystal blue gaze locked on his, one eyebrow beautifully raised. "Oh, no you don't. You can't just throw out an accusation like that and not back it up. Which movies have mistakes?"

She wasn't going to stop 'til she had an answer, but it wouldn't be polite to carry this on without introducing himself. He was just about to when the congressman appeared.

"Ah, you're here," he said, leaning toward Nick and offering his hand. His shake was firm. Too firm. The greeting of a man who always tried to prove himself around other men. They'd met a number of times, and although Nick had thought him insincere and posturing, he wasn't going to argue with what was sure to be a very fat checkbook. "Thank you for being here on such short notice," the congressman said. "Come through to my office."

Nick turned to say good-bye to the woman, kicking himself for not getting her number when he'd had the opportunity. She was standing, too.

"I see you've met," the congressman said, nodding at her.

Nick held out his hand again. "Not properly."

She placed her hand in his, and her grip was firm, that secret smile growing on her mouth as her shining eyes held his. Something kicked in his chest. "Mr. Katsalos has been busy ensuring I don't have unnecessary emotional responses to works of art," she said. "I'm surprised you don't remember me, Nick." She let go and stood straight with her hands clasped in front as if she were about to give a sermon in church.

Damn. She knew him? She wasn't an old girlfriend, was she? It wasn't like him to forget women he'd dated, especially someone as beautiful as this. In fact, if he had dated her, what in all hell had he been thinking in letting her go? It bugged him to think she'd carried this whole conversation on without mentioning it.

"I...ah. No, I don't remember you. I'm sorry. Where did we meet?"

"I'm Erin Patterson."

He felt his smile stiffen, and he swallowed. *Patterson? Sonofa—.* "From Patterson Weddings?"

She grinned, nodding slowly, and his expectations for this day went straight from heel clicks to hell no.

"Shall we adjourn to my office?" the congressman said, and chatted with Erin as they walked down a corridor. As he followed behind them, Nick's brain went into overdrive. Erin had known who he was, and she hadn't said a thing. She'd played him, and he hadn't even known it.

Although he hadn't seen her or any of her family in years, the Patterson name had been like a curse in the Katsalos household for as long as he could remember. Their parents had fallen out decades ago, and while the fortunes of the Palace had suffered for years, he'd heard the Pattersons had gone from strength to strength. If they were both here to meet the congressman, who'd won the contract for his daughter's wedding?

"Take a seat," the congressman said when they'd entered the office and he'd moved behind an enormous wooden desk.

Erin sat first and Nick followed. The last time he'd seen her, they must've been sixteen. Although he'd known how high the level of animosity between the families was back then, it hadn't stopped him from asking her on a date. She'd said yes at first, then changed her mind at the last minute—not before he'd bragged to his friends about it, though. She'd said it was because her father had found out, but something in her eyes said otherwise. Maybe she'd just wanted to make a fool out of him. The way she was sitting now, so confident and collected in her power suit with that whisper of a smile on her lips, suggested she intended to do the same thing today. But damn, she was beautiful.

"I'm sure you're wondering why you're here together," the congressman said as he leaned back in his chair. "I have to say that your proposals for my daughter's wedding were both very strong. Mr. Katsalos, Amy was particularly impressed by the menu that you offered, and as she's had a long interest in all things Greek, your food was her preference."

Nick didn't try to suppress his smile. Everyone told him that the biggest consideration for a wedding was the food. It didn't matter if people were married outside or in, somewhere palatial or a barn, it was the food they remembered, and the Palace's menu was exceptional. With his ability to problem solve and limit errors, he clearly had this in the bag.

"Thank you, sir. Leo Panos, my uncle, has won countless awards for his cooking. I'm glad your daughter approved of the menu. I'm sure the guests at her wedding will be equally impressed."

He threw a look at Erin. He'd heard from his sister Yasmin that while Pattersons had a reputation for style and sophistication, they lacked the friendly, family touch that was the Palace's strength. If the congressman's daughter had loved the Palace's food, then they were home free. So why was Erin here? And why was she still looking so confident... and amused?

The congressman turned to her. "While Amy and her mother loved the food at the Aegean Palace, they couldn't stop talking about the chapel that your venue offered. Patterson Weddings has a strong reputation in Summerville, and it would make us very proud to have Amy's ceremony in your chapel."

A bright smile crossed Erin's face and, impossibly, she looked even more perfect.

A headache bit behind his eyes. He couldn't lose this contract. And he most especially couldn't lose it to Erin Patterson.

"We'd be honored to hold Amy's wedding at Patterson's," Erin said. "She mentioned July next year, and we'll make sure she has her choice of date."

"Wait a minute," Nick said, leaning forward. "Do you mean Patterson Weddings has won this contract? That's not what I was expecting when I was invited here this afternoon. I'm sure that if your daughter loves the food at the Palace so much, we can negotiate some changes so we can give her what she wants for the ceremony as well."

The image of the Williams wedding being held at the Palace, the pictures splashed across the society pages and crowds of new couples booking their weddings years into the future began to disintegrate. Not only could the Palace not afford to lose this contract, they couldn't afford for Patterson's to win it. All that free and in-depth publicity for them was sure to put a nail in the Palace's coffin and mean his parents wouldn't get back together, maybe never come home. And the guilt he'd harbored for what they'd sacrificed for him would never go away. The most important thing was to stay focused on logic and fact, emotion only ever got you into trouble.

"That's not what I had in mind," the congressman said. "My Amy is used to getting what she wants, and in this instance it's the food from the Aegean Palace and the ceremony at Patterson's. I'd appreciate it if you could both make that happen."

"No—!"

"No—!"

Nick and Erin spoke as one, and he had to grip the side of his chair to stop himself from leaping to his feet.

"With all due respect, Congressman, The Aegean Palace is a package. We can't divide up bits here and bits there. If Amy has fallen in love with our food, then I'm sure she'll fall in love with our whole venue as well. She could be married in our garden. We can listen to her preferences for the ceremony and do what we can to incorporate them within our venue."

"I'd have to agree with Mr. Katsalos," Erin said in her quiet but firm voice. "Sharing wouldn't be practical. We're thrilled that Amy loves Patterson's chapel as much as we do and we'd be delighted to adapt our existing menus to incorporate the food of her choice at a reception in our restaurant as well." She threw a look at Nick and smiled brightly. "Much easier to create a new menu than build a whole new venue." Her eyes twinkled as she looked into Nick's eyes and smiled. "That could lead to all sorts of...continuity errors."

The congressman leaned closer and clasped his hands together. He lowered his voice and his eyes narrowed. "Being in the business of making dreams come true, I'm sure you both understand that when a woman finds something she likes, she's not going to let anyone take it away from her."

Erin nodded. "I completely understand, sir. We make dreams happen every day at Patterson's and have all the resources to fulfill Amy's wishes. I've been working in wedding halls since I was twelve years old, so I understand that more than most."

There was a barb in that comment so pointed Nick could feel the jab. Erin knew he didn't do this for a real job, and she was driving home for victory. She'd had him by the balls right from the minute he'd walked into the lobby, and it bugged the hell out of him.

"And may I also remind you," the congressman continued, "that this will be the society wedding of the decade in this county, and there will be plenty of publicity for whoever hosts. If neither of you are prepared to compromise, I'll be forced to offer the contract to Georgia Heights Weddings. I'm sure neither of you would like to see that happen." He stood and walked around the side of the desk. "I anticipated this would take some negotiating, so I'm going to leave you alone to work out the logistics. When you've agreed, I have contracts for you both to sign. I'll be back shortly."

When he'd shut the door behind him, Nick turned to Erin and shook his head. She was sitting with her hands in her lap, her mouth curved in the relaxed way that reminded him of a counselor or a Zen Buddhist. "Did you know about this?"

She blew out an even breath and shook her head. "Not

for a second. I assumed, as I suppose you did, that we'd won the contract until I saw you in the lobby."

Nick nodded. "It's clear he doesn't know who he's dealing with. How he could think either of us would agree to something so impossible is beyond me." Logistics were his specialty. He could fix this.

She twisted in her seat, and now Nick noticed how brilliantly bright her eyes were, almost as if there was a light shining from behind her perfect irises. "The answer is simple. We'll just pay you for the use of your chef and compensate you for losing him on the day. We can make sure he and the Palace are acknowledged in any of the publicity that surrounds the wedding." She sat back in her chair as if it were resolved and they'd be out of here in a few minutes.

He didn't try to stop the laugh that erupted unbidden from his throat. Her proposal was so absurd, so completely unworkable that there wasn't a more appropriate response. "And Patterson's gets the magazine spread and all the follow-up business for years after? Over my dead body."

Erin breathed slowly through her nose and stared down one of her family's greatest rivals. It was clear from what he'd said today that Nick Katsalos was very much like his father, Mano—ruthless, focused, and ready to hold a grudge to his grave—but good lord he was toe-curlingly gorgeous.

She'd always thought the term chiseled was an exaggeration, but Nick's features were so breathtaking he could've been handcrafted from priceless Athenian granite. His Greek heritage was undeniable with his bronze skin and deep brown eyes, and the sculpted set of his body beneath his tailored suit hinted at some kind of celestial involvement in its creation. She took an extra breath to steady her pulse.

Nick Katsalos had figured in one of the most influential days of her life, but it was clear he had no memory of it. He wouldn't have known how distraught she was at the elementary school talent show when her father had told her what an embarrassment she was. She'd played piano and sung a song she'd written about a mermaid, and he'd deemed it "excruciating." Nor would Nick know that her father had wished she'd made him proud like Mano Katsalos was of his son, Nick, the winner with his mathematical genius. When she won this wedding from him, she'd prove she could make her father proud when it really counted.

Not only did she remember him as a cocky schoolboy, she'd followed his career through the years. He was a star track athlete as a teenager, but the last she'd heard he was now doing something in the finance sector and making loads of money in the city. She'd seen photos of him in the media, smiling squarely to the camera, his olive skin glowing with health and confidence, and she'd marveled at the fact that he really did seem to be the sort of guy who had it all.

What he didn't have, though, as far as she knew, was any recent experience in or understanding of the wedding business. With the situation they found themselves in she'd exploit that to its limit. It just seemed especially cruel that she wouldn't be able to take her eyes off him while she was doing it.

"Having the wedding at Patterson's while using your chef is the only logical solution," she said, trying to pull her thoughts back from the way he filled out his suit so perfectly to how she was going to solve this.

"Logic doesn't come into it," he said as he held her gaze,

barely concealed irritation flashing in his eyes. They were the color of toffee pudding, warm and brown, and you just knew they'd be bad for your health. "This is about good business and me getting into bed with..." He seemed to freeze as his composure slipped for the first time, and she felt the corners of her mouth twitch at his unfortunate choice of words.

"What I mean is that having to work hand in glove with my family's biggest rival is as far away from good business as I could ever get."

"Then what do you suggest?" she asked. "It's clear Amy wants her wedding in our chapel, and it's obvious that it will be much easier for us to change our menu than have the wedding in two places. No point letting competition get in the way of common sense."

Nick stood and moved to the window then leaned against the sill. There was no hiding the fact he had money and lived a life far removed from the traditional streets of Brentwood Bay. His shirt was so white she'd bet it had only ever been to a dry cleaner, and the perfectly cut jacket he was wearing was straight out of a fashion magazine. She'd heard his parents had been struggling financially, but it looked as though he wasn't suffering. Pity he didn't seem to enjoy much.

"It can't be that hard to find a compromise." He rubbed a hand across his chin. He was clean-shaven, but she could imagine that late in the evening his chin would sport a sexy shadow with stubble that could make a girl's skin tingle... She crossed her ankles and tried to concentrate on what he was saying.

"It's the publicity that's the priority for both of us, right?" he said.

She smiled. Being a businessman, and someone who

couldn't enjoy a piece of art or a movie for the mistakes in them, it made sense that he would only be interested in numbers through the door. Just like her father. But she was different. She'd promised her grandfather, her mother's father, that she'd look after the wedding venue he'd built before his son-in-law took over and turned it into a slick commercial operation.

"Giving a woman the wedding of her dreams would be my first priority," she said.

He lifted an eyebrow, and she held his penetrating gaze.

"So your success is due to your focus on the bride, not the bottom line?"

"Of course we'd be interested in the publicity," she said. "But we'd prefer it if we didn't have to share it with our competitors."

He crossed his arms. "You've got to admit we're much more than competitors."

She sighed. "Would bitter enemies be more truthful?"

"My father still talks about Patterson's winning the contract for a big society wedding from us and your family making his life impossible ever since."

She let out a quiet breath as the importance of winning this contract came rushing back. Her father had only agreed to her taking the general manager's position for a probationary period while he was ill, but winning this could make her job permanent. Being the one who finally put the Katsalos family in their place—especially Nick—would earn her father's respect for the rest of this life and the next.

"If we can't work together, what do you suggest?" he asked, when she didn't respond.

She paused for a moment, wanting a plan completely formed before she put it to him. If she could think of something big enough... Her father had made it very clear that he was taking a gamble on her, and maybe the only way she could quell the doubt he showed in her every day was to take a gamble of her own. "How about a wager?"

His eyes widened, and he stepped away from the window. "You want to bet on your family's business?"

"If I have to." If she won this contract and carried through with the Williams wedding, she knew she'd have his respect forever. And if her father wasn't running things, Faith and Keira might stay. How she longed to be near her sisters again. For so long her family had felt...broken.

Nick moved back toward her, and this time there was a spark in his eyes. "How would it work?" He sounded hungry and determined, and it made her weak in the knees. He'd already made it clear from his art comments that he focused on fact rather than emotion, and if she could expose that as a weakness, she might be home free.

Her scalp tightened as she launched into her plan. "We'd set up a challenge to be judged by someone influential like, say, *Wedding World* magazine—someone Amy and her parents would have faith in. The company whose whole venue is deemed best by an independent judge would get to hold the Williams wedding outright."

He frowned. "How would that work in favor of what Amy wanted, though? She's already said she likes your chapel but our food. What could convince her to go with one place or the other?"

"We could obviously make any changes in the meantime, but we'd have to offer some sort of extra incentive for her father to go with our plan. Maybe the loser could cater the congressman's annual charity dinner for free. He'd love all the publicity that would generate."

Nick scrubbed a hand across his chin. She could see him calculating this, treating it as if it was a movie he was determined to find fault with. "Sounds unconventional to me, but intriguing."

"I guess it is unconventional, but I can't see another solution. And the best part would be that no matter who won, both businesses would get a whole lot of exposure through the coverage of the wager in the magazine, and the winners would, of course, get the grand prize of hosting the wedding and all the publicity." She was surprising even herself with how perfect this sounded.

He tilted his head, and his stare became more intense, more challenging, and goose bumps raced across the back of her neck. "I wasn't expecting you to be the sort of woman who'd take a risk like that."

It was the first personal comment he'd made, and her reply came out too quickly. "What sort of woman did you expect me to be?"

Whether it was the intense way he was looking at her, or the fact there was so much riding on this, Erin didn't know, but for some inexplicable reason her heart rate tripled. She'd been around good-looking guys before, but there was something about Nick Katsalos, something a little dangerous and unpredictable that gave her body a mind of its own. She really shouldn't like that feeling so much.

"What sort of woman?" he asked. "Someone more like the girl I remember. Someone who'd play it safe. Someone who'd take the easy option and bow out when it all got too hard."

So he did remember her. Not from the talent show, she was sure, more likely the time she'd changed her mind when he'd asked her out years later. She'd said it was because her father had found out, but in reality he'd been forbidden fruit back then, and just as if he was the last chocolate in the box, he'd become the focus of her desire once too often. Her lack of faith in her ability to stop herself from falling for him had been the real reason. Things were different now. Now she had more riding on this than he ever would, and she didn't intend to lose.

"Then it goes to prove that just like your understanding of art and a good movie, it's your perceptions that are faulty," she said with a smile. "I want this contract more than I've wanted anything in my life, but I intend to fight fair for it. You're right that nothing good can come out of us sharing the Williams wedding." So he'd expected her to roll over and give in? He was in for a nasty surprise.

He'd moved closer. She could see in his eyes how much this challenge excited him, and she had to admit it excited her, too. The feud between their families settled, her position as general manager at Patterson's secured, her father's approval guaranteed, and her sisters close by, each was just as much of a prize as winning this contract. "And if you lost, you'd be prepared to bow out gracefully?" he asked as he drew level with her chair.

"I'm not going to lose."

His lips tipped in a grin. An infuriatingly sexy, confident grin, and all the blood rushed to her cheeks. "You're not just making a point with a wager?"

She cleared her throat. She'd thought she was in control of this, suggesting the wager and the terms of it, and now he'd switched it so he was the one questioning her motives. The memory of the talent show exploded in her mind. Nick Katsalos wouldn't show her up ever again. "Of course not."

The smile increased, and he flashed beautifully white teeth. "When you first mentioned it, I thought you were crazy, but now it makes perfect sense. I only ever take a chance on sure things, and I think this is one. In fact, I'm so sure, I'm going to up the stakes on your wager. I'm going to offer the services of our chef for a year free of charge if we lose."

Her mouth dried. He couldn't be serious. Leo Panos was an amazing chef. Wedding guests at Patterson's often asked if they could provide food more like what was on offer at the Palace, but they never got it quite right. Her father was a notoriously difficult boss, and they hadn't been able to hold onto good staff. If they had Leo, that final part of the business puzzle would be in place, and there would be no stopping them. "You'd pay his salary for a year?"

He nodded slowly as if he held every one of the cards she'd just dealt, and a realization of what the stakes were hit like a kettle ball to her stomach.

"It might take a bit to convince him to leave the Palace, but yes, I'd offer him double the salary to work for you for a year, and it wouldn't cost Patterson's a dime. When the year was up, he'd come back to us."

"You must be pretty confident you'll win if you're upping the stakes so much," she said, trying to keep her voice even. She wasn't quite sure how it had happened, but it felt as though she'd gone from almost having the contract to Nick Katsalos telling her she had no hope in hell. She needed to remind herself that Amy Williams had loved much of what they had to offer and she was certain *Wedding World* would, too. The alternative was too frightening to think about.

"I am. Extremely confident." He grinned slowly. "And you?"

She couldn't leave him with the upper hand, couldn't have him thinking he had some sort of psychological power over her. "Confident enough that I can offer stakes far higher than a chef for a year."

Her mouth dried, and she tried to swallow past the tightness in her throat. *Could she? What on Earth would it be? Why had she let the smooth and sexy Nick Katsalos get under her skin?* He'd suggested she was tougher than he'd expected—well, maybe she needed to show him just how tough she could be. After all, that's exactly what she needed to prove to her father. She looked around, as if out of nowhere she could conjure something so priceless, so worthy that he'd realize just what he was up against.

"And what treasure might that be?" he asked, grinning, and all she could think of was the desperate need to wipe that self-satisfied grin off his face.

"The Patterson Weddings logo." As soon as she'd said the words her heart began to trip.

The silence in the room seemed to burn her eardrums until Nick gave a long, low whistle. "The iron logo on the entrance archway? The symbol that has taunted my father for decades? That's one helluva raise."

Oh God. Had she really bet that? There was no backing down now. She lifted her chin. "Exactly. If we lose, you can come by and remove the Patterson Weddings logo with your bare hands, and your father will have his victory once and for all."

Was she mad? Her father would have a fit if he knew what she was betting. But as she looked at the smiling challenge in Nick's eyes, she remembered that she wasn't going to let him triumph ever again. She'd put absolutely everything in to winning this wager.

"Them's fighting words," he said, and then his teeth flashed in a full-blown smile. "I'm impressed, Erin. I think we have a competition on our hands. I can't wait to toast the winner with the finest champagne there is."

She shrugged as if this conversation was nothing more than a polite exchange on a sunny summer's day. Inside, her stomach was tangled into a fist of fear. "It will all be moot anyway," she said, trying to imagine the look on her father's face if he ever found out she'd gambled with the symbol of his greatest achievement. She was determined to stay focused on the only outcome she could live with: she as the respected general manager of Patterson Weddings, her family together once and for all, and the feud with the Katsalos family over for good. She made herself smile back at him. "Patterson's will win," she said. "You won't find any mistake about that."

You can buy **Winning the Wedding War** here, or ask for it at your book store or local library.

GET A FREE NOVELLA

Throughout my career, my readers have been such a key part of my writing life and I love to keep them up to date with what I'm doing. I occasionally send out newsletters with details on new releases and extra special offers for both my books and those like mine. I promise I won't bombard you!

If you sign up to the reader list, the first thing I'll send you is a **FREE** novella, *Waiting on Forever*, the prequel to my *Tall, Dark and Driven* series.

One last task to complete, then Alex Panos can fulfil a heart breaking promise. That is, if he can get past cute and quirky Mara Hemmingway.

On her own since she was sixteen, Mara won't be taken advantage of again—especially not by brooding and troubled Alex. Instead, she'll play him at his own game.

When their powerful attraction threatens to get in the way of both their dreams, someone will have to face a future of waiting on forever.

You can claim your **FREE** novella here or email barb@barbaradeleo.com.

LOVE BARBARA'S BOOKS?

JOIN BARBARA'S ARC REVIEW TEAM!

Barbara is currently taking applications to join her ARC review team.

Being on Barbara's ARC team means you'll have access to exclusive content, you'll have early access to new books before anyone else, and you'll be able to review her books early.

All members of Barbara's ARC team also receive exclusive content including the family tree and a list of all titles for her **Tall, Dark and Driven** series.

Fill out an ARC reader team application form here, or email barb@barbaradeleo.com and Barbara will be in touch!

ABOUT BARBARA

Multi award winning author, Barbara DeLeo's first book, co-written with her best friend, was a story about beauty queens in space. She was eleven, and the sole, handwritten copy was lost years ago much to everyone's relief. It's some small miracle that she kept the faith and now lives her dream of writing sparkling contemporary romance with unforgettable characters.

Degrees in English and Psychology, and a career as an English teacher, fueled Barbara's passion for people and stories, and a number of years living in Europe —primarily in Athens, Greece—gave her a love for romantic settings.

Discovering she was having her second set of twins in two years, Barbara knew she must be paying penance for being disorganized in a previous life and now uses every spare second to create her stories.With every word she writes, Barbara is sharing her belief in the transformational power of loving relationships.

Married to her winemaker hero for twenty two years, Barbara's happiest when she's getting to know her latest cast of characters. She still loves telling stories about finding love in all the wrong places, but now without a beauty queen or spaceship in sight.

ALSO BY BARBARA DELEO

The Tall, Dark and Driven series

All books can be read as stand alone.

Waiting on Forever—prequel novella ~ **Alex's story** ~ available **FREE** here or email barb@barbaradeleo.com

Winning the Wedding War —**Book 2** ~ **Nick's story** available here or ask for it at your local book store or library.

Reining in the Rebel—**Book 3** ~ **Ari's story** available here or ask for it at your local book store or library.

A Home for Summer—**Book 4** ~ **Costa's story**

available here or ask for it at your local book store or library.

A Marriage for Show—**Book 5** ~ **Christo's story**

available here or ask for it at your local book store or library.

A Family for Good—**Book 6** ~ **Markus's story**

available here or ask for it at your local book store or library.

———————————

The Breaking Through series
All books can be read as stand alone.

This series is available on Amazon and Kindle Unlimited, or ask for it at your local book store or library.

Bad Reputations—Book 1 ~ Kirin's story

available here or ask for it at your local book store or library.

For Jay and Luca—two of my most favorite heroes

Making the Love List
A Tall, Dark and Driven book
Yasmin's Story

by Barbara DeLeo

This book is a work of fiction. Names, characters, places and incidents are the product of the author's imagination or are used fictitiously. Any resemblance to actual events, locales, or persons, living or dead, is coincidental.

This book was previously published, in part, as The Bouquet List

Cover Design - Natasha Snow Designs www.natashasnow.com

ACKNOWLEDGMENTS

Not only was I lucky enough to have been born into a wonderfully supportive family where dreams are championed and crazy little quirks celebrated, I've been welcomed into a second family too. Since I met my Greek boyfriend, now husband, thirty years ago, I've been immersed in a culture, a language, and a way of celebrating life that I love. I'd like to thank both families for giving me love, laughter, and inspiration for the story of the Katsalos family in my *Tall, Dark and Driven* series.

My heartfelt thanks also goes to:

My agent, Nalini Akolekar, who always has my back and wonderful advice to share.

My incredible crit partners, Hayson Manning and Rachel Bailey, who are amazing writers and save my patootie time and time again.

Iona, Sue, Kate, Courtney, Deborah and Nadine who are the BEST group of motivators, cheerleaders and wine drinking pals a girl could have.

My cover designer, Natasha Snow, who nails it every time.

My proofreader Amy Hart.

And to George and my four amazing children, thank you for helping me to keep on living this dream. Squeeze, squeeze, squeeze.

Barb X

Manufactured by Amazon.ca
Bolton, ON